Fergus   Hume

Monsieur Judasx

Fergus Hume

Monsieur Judasx

ISBN/EAN: 9783337364205

Printed in Europe, USA, Canada, Australia, Japan

Cover: Foto ©Andreas Hilbeck / pixelio.de

More available books at **www.hansebooks.com**

Transcriber's Notes:

    1. Original text provided by Walter Moore for Project Gutenberg Australia.
http://gutenberg.net.au/ebooks17/1700671h.html

    2. Publication date is 1891 per British Museum Catalogue of Printed Books page
491—https://books.google.com/books?id=_5ghAQAAMAAJ&pg

Monsieur Judas

A Paradox

by

Fergus Hume

London:
Spencer Blackett
[1891]

CONTENTS

3

Chapter 1

The Jarlchester Mystery

Not an important place by any means, this sleepy little town lying at the foot of a low range of undulating hills, beside a slow-flowing river. A square-towered church of Norman architecture, very ancient and very grim; one principal narrow street, somewhat crooked in its course; other streets, narrower and more crooked, leading off on the one side to the sheltering hills, and on the other down to the muddy stream. Market-place octagonal in shape, with a dilapidated stone cross of the Plantagenet period in the centre; squat stone bridge, with massive piers, across the sullen gray waters; on the farther shore a few red-roofed farmhouses; beyond, fertile pastoral lands and the dim outline of distant hills.

Picturesque in a quiet fashion certainly, but not striking in any way; a haven of rest for worn-out people weary of worldly troubles, but dull—intensely dull—for visionary youth longing for fame. The world beyond did not know

4

Jarlchester, and Jarlchester did not know the world beyond, so accounts were thus equally balanced between them.

Being near Winchester, the ancient capital of Saxon England, it was asserted by archaeologists that Jarlchester, sleepy and dull as it was in the nineteenth century, had once been an important place. Jarl means Earl, and Chester signifies a camp; so those wiseacres asserted that the name Jarlchester meant the Camp of the Earl; from which supposition arose a fable that Jarl Godwin had once made the little town his head-quarters when in revolt against pious Edward who built St. Peter's of Westminster. As Godwin, however, according to history, never revolted against the King, and generally resided in London, the authenticity of the story must be regarded as doubtful. Nevertheless, Jarlchester folks firmly believed in it, and sturdily held to their belief against all evidence to the contrary, however clearly set forth.

They were a sleepy lot as a rule, those early-to-bed and early-to-rise country folk; for nothing had occurred for years to disturb their sluggish minds, so they had gradually sunk into a state of somnolent indifference, with few ideas beyond the weather and the crops.

Then Jarlchester, unimportant since Anglo-Saxon times, suddenly became famous throughout England on account of "The Mystery," and the mystery was "A Murder."

On this moist November morning, when the whole earth shivered under a bleak gray sky, a crowd, excited in a dull, bovine way, was assembled in front of the "Hungry Man Inn," for in the commercial-room thereof, now invested with a ghastly interest, an inquest was being held on the body of a late guest of the inn, and the bucolic crowd was curious to know the verdict.

A long, low-ceilinged apartment this commercial-room, with a narrow deal table covered with a glaring red cloth down the centre; four tall windows looking out on to the crowd, who, with faces flattened against the glass, peered into the room. A jury of lawful men and true, much impressed with a sense of their importance, seated at the narrow table; at the top thereof, the coroner, Mr. Carr, bluff, rosy-faced, and eminently respectable. Near him a slender young man, keen-eyed and watchful, taking notes (reported by the crowd outside to be a London detective); witnesses seated here, there, and everywhere among eager spectators; but the body! oh, where was the body, which was the culminating point of interest in the whole gruesome affair? The crowd outside was visibly disappointed to learn that the body was lying upstairs in a darkened room, and the jury, half eager, half fearful, having inspected it according to precedent, were now assembled to hear all procurable evidence as to the mode in which the living man of two days ago became the body upstairs.

First Witness.—Boots. Short, grimy, bashful; pulls forelock stolidly, shuffles with his feet, is doubtful as to aspirates, and speaks hoarsely, either from cold—it is raining—or from nervousness either of the jury or of the body; perhaps both.

"Name? Jim Bulkins, sir. Bin boots at "Ungry Man' fur two year'n more come larst Easter. Two days back, gen'man— him upstair—come 'ere t' stay. Come wi' couach fro' Winchester. Ony a bag—leather bag—very light. Carried 't upstair fur gen'man, who 'ad thir'-seven. Gen'man come 'bout five. 'Ad dinner, then wrote letter. Posted letter hisself. Show'd 'im post orfice. Guv me sixpence; guv me t'other fur carr'in' up bag. Seemed cheerful. Went t' bed 'bout nine. Nex' mornin' I went upstair with butts. Gen'man arsked fur butts t' be givin pusonally t' 'im 'cause 'e were perticler 'bout

6

polish. Knocked at door; n' anser. Knocked agin; n' anser. Thought gen'man 'sleep, so pushed door to put butts inside; door were open."

Coroner.—"What do you mean by the door being open?"

Witness.—"Weren't locked, sir; closed t' a bit—what you might call ajar, sir. Entered room, put down butts; gen'man were lyin' quiet in bed. Thought 'e were sleepin' an' come downstair. This were 'bout nine. At ten went up agin. Knocked; n' anser. Knocked agin; n' anser. Went into room agin; gen'man still sleepin'. Went to wake 'im an' found 'e were ded. Sung out at onct, an' Mr. Chickles 'e come up."

Juryman (sharp-nosed and inquisitive).—"How was he lying when you saw him first?"

Witness.—"Bedclose up t' chin, sir. 'Ands and h'arms inside bedclose; lyin' on back—bedclose smooth like. Know'd 'e were ded by whiteness of 'is face—like chalk, sir—h'awful!"

Coroner.—"Are you sure deceased asked you to give him his boots personally next morning?"

Witness.—"Yes, sir—said 'e were vury perticler."

Coroner.—"Did he seem to you like a man intending to make away with himself?"

Witness.—"No, sir. Quite lively like. Sed as 'ow 'e were goin' to look roun' this 'ole nex' day, sir."

Coroner (pompously).—"And what did the deceased mean by the expression 'this hole,' my man?"

Witness (grinning).—"Jarlchester, sir."

7

Great indignation on the part of the patriotic jury at hearing their native town thus described, and as Boots is still grinning, thinking such remark to be an excellent joke, he is told sharply to stand down, which he does with obvious relief.

The next witness called was Sampson Chickles, the landlord of the "Hungry Man." A fat, portly individual is Mr. Chickles, with a round red face, and a ponderous consciousness that he is the hero of the hour—or rather the minute. "Swear Sampson Chickles!" Which is done by a fussy clerk with a rapid gabble and a dingy Bible—open at Revelations—and Mr. Chickles, being sworn to tell the truth and nothing but the truth, gives his evidence in a fat voice coming somewhere from the recesses of his rotund stomach.

"My name, gentlemen, is Sampson Chickles, and I've lived in Jarlchester, man and boy, sixty years. But I keep my health wonderful, gentlemen, saving a touch of the—"

Coroner.—"Will the witness kindly confine himself to the matter in hand?"

Witness (somewhat ruffled).—"Meaning the dead one, I presume, Mr. Carr. Certainly, Mr. Carr; I was coming to that. He—meaning the dead one—came here two days ago by the coach from Winchester. There is, gentlemen, no name on his bag—there is no name on his linen—no letters, no cards in his pockets—not even initials, gentlemen, to prevent his clothes being stolen at the wash. He never mentioned his name, Mr. Carr. I was going to ask him next morning, but he was dead, and therefore, gentlemen, not in a position to speak. As far as I am concerned, Mr. Carr, the dead one has never been christened. The mystery—meaning the dead one—has no name that I ever heard of, and was spoken of by me and my daughter (who may know more

8

than her father) as the gentleman in No. 37. I only spoke to the dead one twice, Mr. Carr and gentlemen; once when I arranged about terms—thirty shillings a week, gentlemen, not including wine—and again when I asked him if he had enjoyed his dinner—soup, fish, fowl, and pudding. Gentlemen, he had enjoyed his dinner."

A Juryman (hungry-looking, evidently thinking of the dinner).—"Was he cheerful, Mr. Chickles?"

Witness.—"Jocund, sir, if I may use the term. Merry as a lark."

Facetious juryman suggests wine.

Witness (with mournful dignity).—"No, sir! Pardon me, Mr. Specks, he had no wine while he was in this house. His explanation was a simple one, gentlemen—wine did not agree with his pills—tonic pills, Mr. Carr—one to be taken before bedtime every night."

Coroner (with the air of having found something).—"Pills, eh? Did he look ill?"

Witness.—"Not exactly ill, Mr. Carr; not exactly well, gentlemen. Betwixt and between. Weak, sir. His legs shook, his hands trembled, and when a door banged he jumped, gentlemen—jumped!"

A Juryman.—"Then I presume he was taking tonic pills for his constitution?"

Witness.—"Well, yes, Mr. Polder, yes, sir. There is the box of pills—tonic pills, as he—meaning the dead one—told me. Found in his room, gentlemen—on the chest of drawers— after his death."

Inspection of pills by jury. Great curiosity evinced when pills (eight in number) appeared to be like any other pills. The London detective, however, secured the pill-box after inspection, and sat with it in his hand thinking deeply.

Mr. Chickles, having given all his evidence, retired, with the full consciousness that he had given it in a masterly fashion; and his daughter, Miss Molly Chickles, plump, pretty, and a trifle coquettish, was duly sworn. At first she was rather bashful, but having found her tongue—a task of little difficulty for this rustic daughter of Eve—told all she knew with many sidelong glances and confused blushes—feminine arts not quite thrown away on the jury, although they were to a man married and done for.

Said Molly, in answer to the Coroner:

"My name is Mary Chickles. Father calls me Molly. I am the daughter of Sampson Chickles, and barmaid here. I knew the deceased, but he did not tell me his name. He arrived here two days ago—on Tuesday, at five, by the coach. He came into the bar, and asked me if he could put up here for a week. I told him he could, and called father, who arranged about the terms. He then went up to his bedroom and came down to dinner at six. After dinner he went into the parlour, and I think wrote a letter. After doing so he asked me where the post office was. I sent him with Boots, and heard afterwards that he posted his letter. On his return he sat down in the bar for a few minutes. There was no one there at the time. He seemed to me to be very weak, and told me his nerves were shattered. I asked him if he had consulted a doctor. He replied that he had done so, and was taking tonic pills every night before he went to bed. I said that I hoped he took them regular, as it was no use unless he did so. He assured me that he always took one pill every night without fail. He mentioned that he was going to stay

10

for a time in Jarlchester, and hoped the quiet would do him good."

Coroner. — "Did he say he was down here for his health?"

Witness. — "Not exactly, sir; but he talked a good deal about his nerves, and such like. He said he was going to stay a week or so, and expected a friend to join him shortly."

Coroner. — "Oh! a friend, eh! Man or woman?"

Witness. — "He did not say, sir."

A Juryman. — "When did he expect this friend?"

Witness. — "He said in a few days, but did not mention any special time. After a short conversation he went to bed at nine o'clock, and next morning father told me he was dead."

Coroner. — "Did he appear gloomy or low-spirited?"

Witness. — "Oh, dear no, sir. A very pleasant-spoken gentleman. He said his nerves were bad, but I was quite astonished at his cheerfulness."

Coroner. — "Did he say anything about the next day?"

Witness. — "Yes, sir. He asked if there was anything to be seen in Jarlchester, and when I told him about the church, he said he would look it up next day."

A Juryman. — "Do you think he had any intention of destroying himself?"

Witness. — "Not so far as I saw, sir."

Coroner. — "He did not mention anything about the letter?"

Witness.—"Not a word, sir."

A Juryman (facetiously).—"Did you think him good-looking, Miss Molly?"

Witness (tossing her head).—"Well, not what I call handsome, sir; but there's no knowing what other girls think."

With this parting shot, Miss Chickles retired to her usual place in the bar, and gossiped to outsiders about the present aspect of the case, while Sergeant Spills, the head of the Jarlchester police force, came forward to give his evidence. A crisp, dry-looking man, the Sergeant, with a crisp, dry manner, and a sharp ring in the tones of his voice; economical in his words, decisive in his speech.

"Charles Spills, sir, sergeant of the police in Jarlchester. Jim Bulkins reported death of deceased. Came here, saw body lying in bed. Clothes drawn up to chin. In my opinion, deceased died in his sleep. Examined bag of deceased. Contained linen (not marked), suit of clothes (not marked), toilet utensils of the usual kind. Drawing block and some lead pencils (much used)."

Coroner (prompted by London detective).—"Were there any drawings?"

Witness.—"No, sir."

Coroner.—"No sketches or faces on the block?"

Witness.—"No, sir! Clothes worn by deceased—dark blue serge suit, double-breasted."

Coroner.—"Any name on the clothes?"

Witness.—"No, sir! Tag used to hang up coat, on which tailor's name generally placed, torn off. Searched pockets; found penknife, loose silver (twelve shillings and sixpence), and box of pills laid before the jury. Silver watch on dressing-table—silver chain attached—silver sovereign purse containing six sovereigns. Nothing else."

Coroner.—"Nothing likely to lead to the name of deceased?"

Witness.—"Absolutely nothing, sir. Searched, but found no name. Inquired—discovered no name. Case puzzled me, so wired to London for detective—Mr. Fanks—now sitting on your left."

Sergeant Spills having thus discharged his duty, saluted in a wooden fashion, and substituting Joe Staggers, coachman, for himself, took up a rigid attitude beside him, like a toy figure in a Noah's ark.

Evidence of Joe Staggers. Horsey gentleman, large, red, and fat; smothered voice, suggestive of drink; a god on the box-seat behind four horses, but a mere mortal given to drink when on the ground.

"Joseph Staggers, sur. 'Ees, sur! Druv the coaach fro Winchester t' Jarlchest'r these ten year an' more. Two days ago—it were Toosd'y, cos t' bay 'oss cast a shoe—I were waitin' at station, an' gen'man—the corpus—come up t' me, an' ses 'e, 'Jarlchest'r?' inquiring like. "Ees, sur,' ses I, an' up 'e gits an' off we goes. 'E sat aside me an' talked of plaace. 'Ees, sur. Ses 'e: 'This are foine arter Lunnon.'"

Coroner.—"Oh, did he say he had come from London?"

Witness (doggedly).—"'E ses what I sed afore, sur. Talked foine, sur; but didn't knaw a 'oss fro' a cow."

Mr. Staggers' evidence unanimously pronounced by jury to be worse than useless, an opinion not shared by Mr. Fanks (of London, detective), who scratched down something in a secretive little book with a vicious little pencil.

Coroner. — "Call Dr. Drewey."

A most important witness, Dr. Drewey, he having made a post-mortem examination of the body, and the jury, hitherto somewhat languid, now wake up, Mr. Fanks turns over a new page in his secretive little book, and Dr. Drewey, bland, gentlemanlike, in a suit of sober black, and gravely smiling (professional smile), gives his opinion of things with great unction.

"I have examined the body of the deceased. It is that of a man of about eight-and-twenty years of age. Very badly nourished, and with comparatively little food in the stomach. The stomach itself was healthy, but I found the vessels of the head unusually turgid throughout. There was also great fluidity of the blood, and serous effusion in the ventricles. The pupils of the eyes were much contracted. Judging from these appearances, and from the turgescence of the vessels of the brain, I have no hesitation in declaring that the deceased died from an overdose of morphia or of opium."

Coroner. — "Then you think the deceased took an overdose of poison?"

Witness (with bland reproof). — "I say he died from an overdose, but I am not prepared to say that he took it himself."

A Juryman. — "Then some one administered the dose?"

14

Witness.—"I can't say anything about that."

A Juryman.—"When do you think the deceased died?"

Witness.—"That is a very difficult question to answer. In most cases of poisoning by opium, death takes place within from six to twelve hours. I examined the body of the deceased between one and two o'clock the next day, and from all appearances he had been dead ten hours. According to the evidence of Miss Chickles, he went to bed at nine o'clock, so if he took the dose of opium then—as was most likely—he must have died about four o'clock in the morning."

Coroner.—"During his sleep?"

Witness.—"Presumably so, opium being a narcotic."

Coroner (prompted by London detective).—"Did his stomach look like that of an habitual opium-eater?"

Witness.—"No, not at all."

Coroner.—"According to you, the deceased must have taken the poison at nine o'clock when he went to bed, and on looking at the evidence of Miss Chickles, I see that the deceased stated that he took his tonic pill regularly before he went to bed. Now did it strike you that he might have taken two pills by mistake, which would account for his death?"

Witness (hesitating).—"I acknowledge that such an explanation certainly did occur to me, and I analysed three pills selected at random from the box. When I did so, I found it was impossible such pills could have caused his death."

Coroner (obviously bewildered).—"Why so?"

15

Witness. — "Because these tonic pills contain arsenic. There is not a grain of morphia to be found in them. If the deceased had died from an overdose of these pills, I would have found traces of arsenic in his stomach; but as he died from the effects of morphia or opium—I am not prepared to say which—these tonic pills have nothing to do with his death."

This decisive statement considerably puzzled the jury. The deceased died of an overdose of morphia, the pills contained nothing but arsenic; so it being clearly proved that the pills had nothing to do with the death, the deceased must have obtained morphia or opium in some other fashion. Sergeant Spills was recalled on the chance that the deceased might have purchased poison from the Jarlchester chemist. In his evidence, however, Sergeant Spills stated that he had, by direction of Dr. Drewey, inquired into the matter, and had been assured by the chemist that the deceased had never been near the shop. The room had been thoroughly searched, and no drugs nor medicine of any kind had been discovered except the box of tonic pills now before the jury. There was absolutely nothing to show how the deceased had come by his death, that is, he had died of an overdose of morphia, but how the morphia had come into his possession was undiscoverable, so the jury were quite bewildered.

All obtainable evidence having been taken, the Coroner gave his opinion thereon in a neat speech, but a speech which showed how undecided he was in his own mind as to the real facts of this peculiar case.

"I think, gentlemen, that you will agree with me in acknowledging this affair to be a remarkably mysterious one. The deceased comes down here from London (as proved by the evidence of Joseph Staggers) for a few days' rest (evidence of Miss Chickles). He gives no name, and has

16

neither name nor initials marked on his linen, his bag, or his clothes. Not even a letter or a card to throw light on his identity. Entirely unknown, he enters the doors of this inn; entirely unknown, he dies the next morning, carrying the secret of his name and his position into the next world. From all accounts (testified by the evidence of several witnesses), he was quite cheerful, and evidently—I cannot be sure—but evidently had no idea of committing suicide. Looking at the question broadly, gentlemen, the idea of suicide would no doubt have to be abandoned; but looking at the case from my point of view, the whole affair is peculiarly suggestive of self-destruction. This gentleman, now deceased, comes down here, he is careful to give no address, which showed that he wished his friends to remain ignorant of his death. He is very cheerful, and talks about exploring the neighbourhood next day—a mere blind, gentlemen of the jury, as I firmly believe. After writing a letter—doubtless one of farewell to some friend—he retires quietly to bed, and is found dead next morning. The post-mortem examination, undertaken by Dr. Drewey, shows that he died from the effects of an overdose of morphia or opium. Now, gentlemen, he must have taken the morphia or opium himself. No one else could have administered it, as he was not known in Jarlchester, having been here only a few hours when his death occurred, so no one had any reason to give him poison. Regarding the pills now before us, they have been analysed by Dr. Drewey, and are found to contain only arsenic, so we may dismiss the pills altogether. He died of morphia and must have taken it himself, as, had it been administered violently by another person, the sounds of a struggle would have been heard. No sounds were heard, however, so this proves to my mind that he killed himself wilfully. No traces of any drugs (saving the pills alluded to) were found in his room; as proved by Sergeant Spills, he bought no drugs from our local chemist, so only one presumption remains. The deceased must have brought here from London a sufficient quantity of morphia to kill him— took it all, and died leaving no trace of the drug behind. Unknown, unnamed, unfriended, the deceased came to this town, and no one but himself could have administered the poison of which he died. You, gentlemen, as well as myself, have heard the evidence of the intelligent witnesses, and will, therefore, give your verdict in accordance with their evidence; but from what has been stated, and from the whole peculiar circumstances of the case, I firmly believe—in my own mind, gentlemen—that the deceased died by his own hand."

Thus far the sapient Coroner, who delivered this address with a solemn air, much to the satisfaction of the jury, who were dull-minded men, quite prepared to be guided by a master-spirit such as they regarded the Coroner.

During the speech, indeed, a scornful smile might have been seen on the thin lips of Mr. Fanks; but no one noticed it, so intent were they on the words of wisdom which fell from the lips of Mr. Coroner Carr.

Under the inspiration, therefore, of the Coroner, the twelve lawful men and true brought in a verdict quite in accordance with their own and the Coroner's ideas on the subject:

"That the deceased (name unknown) died on the morning of the 13th of November, through an overdose of morphia taken by himself during a temporary fit of insanity."

Having thus relieved their minds to their own satisfaction, this assemblage of worthies—asinine for the most part— went their several ways quite convinced that they had solved the Jarlchester Mystery.

"The fools," said Mr. Fanks, scornfully, slipping the pill-box, which had been left on the table, into his pocket. "They think they've got to the bottom of this affair. Why, they don't know what they're talking about."

"You don't think it's suicide?" asked Sergeant Spills, crisply, rather nettled at the poor opinion Mr. Fanks entertained of the Jarlchester brains.

"No, I don't," retorted the detective, coolly; "but I think it's a murder, and an uncommonly clever murder, too."

"But your reasons?" demanded Spills, with wooden severity.

"Ah, my reasons," replied Mr. Fanks, reflectively. "Well, yes! I've got my reasons, but they wouldn't be intelligible to you."

Extracts From a Detective's Note-Book

"A curious case, this Jarlchester Mystery—I must confess myself puzzled . . . From Drewey's evidence deceased died of morphia . . . Pills only contain arsenic . . . can't be any connection between the death and those pills . . . Can't find out where deceased purchased morphia . . . Perhaps Coroner right, and he brought it from London . . . Examined clothes of deceased . . . well made . . . fashionable . . . shabby . . . Qy., seedy swell? . . . such a one might commit suicide . . . Doubtful as to nerve . . .

". . . Don't understand that open door . . . ajar . . . nervous man wouldn't sleep with door ajar . . . absurd . . . Qy., could any one have entered room during night? . . . Impossible, as deceased a stranger here . . .

"*Mem.*—To find out if any one slept in adjacent rooms.

". . . Examine pill-box . . . sudden idea about same . . . Fancy I'll be able to find name of deceased ... if so look for motive of murder . . . questionable, very! if idea will lead to anything . . . still I'll try . . . This case piques my curiosity . . . Is it murder or suicide? . . . I must discover which . . ."

Chapter 2

A Curious Coincidence

That night, after a comfortable dinner—and the "Hungry Man's" dinners were something to be remembered—Mr. Fanks sat in front of the fire staring into a chaos of burning coals, and thinking deeply. It was in the commercial-room, of course, but there were no commercial travellers present. Mr. Fanks with a world of thought in his shrewd face was the only occupant of the room, and sat within the cheery circle of light proceeding from the red glare of the fire and the yellow flame of the lamp, while at his back the place was in semi-darkness. Cold, too—a nipping, chilly, frosty feeling, as if winter was giving the world a foretaste of his Christmas quality, and outside on the four tall windows beat the steady rain, while occasionally a gust of wind made their frames rattle.

Here, however, in this oasis of light in a desert of gloom, everything was pleasant and agreeable, except perchance Mr. Fanks, who sat with his cup of coffee standing on the table at his elbow untasted, while he frowned thoughtfully at the chaotic fire as though he had a personal spite against it.

A clever face, a very clever face, clean shaven, with sharply cut features, dark hair, touched with gray at the temples, and cut short in the military fashion, keen eyes of a bluish tint, with a shrewd twinkle in their depths, and a thin-lipped, resolute mouth—perhaps a trifle too resolute for so young a man (he was not more than thirty); but then, Mr. Fanks, although young in years, was old in experience, and every line on his features was a record of something learned at the cost of something lost, and on that account never forgotten. A smart, alert figure, too, had Mr. Fanks, well-clothed in a rough gray tweed suit, slender, sinewy hands with a ring—signet ring—on the little finger of the left one, and well-formed feet, neatly shod in boots of tanned leather.

A gentleman! Yes, decidedly the London detective was a gentleman—that could be seen by his whole appearance; and as to his dress, well, he wore his clothes like a man who went to a good tailor and valued him accordingly.

Quoth Mr. Fanks, after some minutes of deep thought, during which he removed his keen eyes from gazing fire-wards, and looked doubtfully at a pill-box which he held in his left hand:

"This is the only clue I can possibly obtain. The chemist who made up these pills has kindly put his name and address—in print—on the box. If, then, I go to this chemist, I will be able to find out the name of the dead man—after that the circumstances of his life, and then—well, after all, I may be wrong, and these country bumpkins right. It may be a case of suicide—I suppose, under the circumstances, they could hardly bring in any other verdict, and yet it is so strange. Why should he have poisoned himself with morphia, when he could have done so with an overdose of

21

these pills? Easier death, I dare say. Morphia is a narcotic, and arsenic an irritant. Humph! it's a strange case altogether—very strange. I don't know exactly what to make of it."

He relapsed into silence, slipped the pill-box into his pocket, and taking the cup from the table began to sip his coffee slowly. Coffee—black coffee, hot and strong, as Mr. Fanks was now taking it—clears the brain, and renders it intensely sharp and wakeful; so after a few minutes the detective put down the cup, and thrusting his hands into his trousers pockets, stretched out his long legs, and began to think aloud once more, as was his fashion when alone.

"It's a fine profession that of a detective, but one gets tired of commonplace murders; this, however, isn't a commonplace murder. Query. Is it a murder at all? Jury say 'No.' I say 'Yes'—eh! I wonder who is right! Egotism on my part, probably, but I believe in my own idea. Why should a man come down to this out-of-the-way place to die? Why should he take the trouble to explain that he intends to stop here for a week if he intended to commit suicide? No! I can't and won't believe it's suicide. As to that theory of Carr's, that he brought just enough morphia to poison himself. Rubbish! Suicides don't take so much trouble as a rule. My belief," continued Mr. Fanks, reflectively, "my belief is that he took something innocently and it killed him. Now what would he take innocently? These pills, of course! Yet, if they killed him, it would be arsenic, not morphia. Hang it, what the deuce does it all mean?"

There being no answer to this question, he caught his chin between his finger and thumb, staring hard at the fire meanwhile, as if thereby to solve his doubts. A hard case, this Jarlchester Mystery; a difficult case; and yet it fascinated Mr. Fanks by its very difficulty. He was fond of difficulties, this young man. In his childish days, Chinese puzzles—most perplexing of mysteries—had been his delight. As a schoolboy, he adored algebraical problems and newspaper cryptograms, so now in his early manhood he found his true vocation in solving those inexplicable enigmas which the criminal classes, and very often the non-criminal classes—principally the latter—present to the world for solution.

Mr. Fanks was suddenly aroused from his problematical musings by the sudden opening of the door, and on turning his head with a start, saw it was being closed by a tall young man, who immediately afterwards advanced slowly towards the fire.

"As this is the warmest room in the house," said the new-comer, carelessly, "I've ventured to intrude my company upon you for an hour or so."

"Very pleased, indeed," murmured Mr. Fanks, pushing his chair to one side, so as to allow the stranger to have a fair share of the fire. "It's dull work sitting alone."

This movement on the part of Mr. Fanks and the sitting down of the stranger brought both their faces within the mellow radiance of the lamp, whereupon a sudden look of recognition flashed into the eyes of each.

"Roger Axton!" cried the detective, springing to his feet.

"Fanks!" said the other, also rising and cordially clasping the hand held out to him. "My dear old schoolfellow!"

"And your dear old schoolfellow's nickname also," remarked Fanks, as they shook hands heartily. "What a curious coincidence, to be sure! It is only the mountains that never meet."

"Ten years ago," said Axton, resuming his seat with a sigh. "Ten years ago, Octavius!"

"And it seems like yesterday," observed Octavius, smiling. "Strange that I should meet little Axton at Jarlchester, of all places in the world. What brought you here, old boy?"

"My own legs," said Roger, complacently. "I'm in the poet trade, and have been trying to draw inspiration from nature during a walking tour."

"A poet, eh! Yes, I remember your rhapsodies about Shelley and Keats at school. So you've followed in their footsteps, Roger. 'The child's the father of the man.' That's the Bible, isn't it?"

"I've got a hazy idea that Wordsworth said something like it," responded Axton, drily. "Yes, I'm a poet. And you?"

"I'm the prose to your poetry. You study nature, I study man."

"Taken Pope's advice, no doubt. A novelist?"

"No; not a paying line nowadays. Overcrowded."

"A schoolmaster?"

"Worse still. We can't all be Arnolds."

"Let us say a phrenologist?"

"Pooh! do I look like a charlatan?"

"No, indeed, Fanks! Eh, Fanks," repeated Axton, struck with a sudden idea, and pushing his chair away from that of his companion. "Why, you're a detective down here about that —that suicide."

"What wonderful penetration!" said Octavius, laughing. "How did you hit upon that idea, my friend?"

Roger Axton's hand went up to his fair moustache, which hardly concealed the quivering of his lips, and he laughed in an uneasy manner.

"Circumstantial evidence," he said at last, hurriedly. "The barmaid told me that a London detective called Fangs was down here on account of the—the suicide, and allowing for her misuse of the name, and your unexpected presence here, it struck me—"

"That I must be the man," finished Fanks, shooting a keen glance at the somewhat careworn face of his school friend. "Well, you are perfectly right. I am Octavius Fanks, of Scotland Yard, detective, formerly Octavius Rixton, of nowhere in particular, idler. You don't seem to relish the idea of my being a bloodhound of the law."

"I—I—er—well, I certainly don't see why a detective shouldn't be as respectable as any other man. Still—"

"There's a kind of Dr. Fell dislike towards him," responded Octavius, composedly. "Yes, that's true enough, though intensely ridiculous. People always seem to be afraid of a detective. I don't know why, unless, maybe, it's their guilty conscience."

"Their conscience?" faltered Axton, with an obvious effort.

"I said 'their guilty conscience'" corrected Fanks, with emphasis. "I'll tell you all about it, Roger. But first take your face out of the shadow, and let me have a look at you. I want to see how the boy of seventeen looks as the man of seven-and-twenty."

Reluctantly—very reluctantly, Roger Axton did as he was requested, and when the yellow light shone full on his face, the detective stared steadily at him, with the keen look of one accustomed to read every line, every wrinkle, every light, every shadow on the features of his fellow-men, and skilled to understand the meanings thereof.

It was a handsome young face of the fresh-coloured Saxon type, but just now looked strangely haggard and careworn. Dark circles under the bright blue eyes, the complexion faded from healthy hues to a dull unnatural white; and the yellow hair tossed in careless disorder from off the high forehead, whereon deep lines between the arched eyebrows betrayed vexation or secret trouble—perhaps both. A face that should have worn a merry smile, but did not; lips that should have shown the white teeth in a happy laugh, but did not; eyes that should have burned with poetic fire, with jocund good-humour, with love fire, but did not. No! this face that was young, and should have looked young, bore the impress of a disturbed mind, of a spirit ill at ease, and the keen-eyed detective, withdrawing his gaze with a sigh from the face, let it rest on the figure of Roger Axton.

No effeminacy there, in spite of the girlish delicacy of the face and the gentle look in the blue eyes. On the contrary, a stalwart, muscular frame, well developed, and heavily knit. Plenty of bone, and flesh, and muscle, over six feet in height, an undefinable look of latent strength, of easy consciousness of power. Yes, Roger Axton was not an antagonist to be despised, and looked more like a fighting man-at-arms than a peaceful poet.

He bore the scrutiny of Mr. Fanks, however, with obvious discomposure, and the hand holding the well-worn briar-root, which he was filling from his tobacco-pouch, trembled slightly in spite of all his efforts to steady the muscles.

26

"Well!" he said at length, striking a match, "I see you bring your detective habits into private life, which must be pleasant for your friends. May I ask if you are satisfied?"

"The face," observed Octavius, leisurely waving his hand to disperse the smoke-clouds rolling from the briar-root of his companion, "the face is not that of a happy man!"

"It would be very curious if it was," replied Axton, sulkily, "seeing that the owner is not happy."

"Youth, good looks, genius, health," said Fanks, reflectively. "With all these you ought to be happy, Roger."

"No doubt! But what I ought to be and what I am, are two very different things."

"Judging by your face, they certainly are," retorted the detective, drily; "but what is the matter with you, grumbler? Are you hard up?"

"No! I have a sufficiency of this world's goods."

"The critics have been abusing your last poems, perhaps?"

"Pooh! I'm used to that."

"Ah! then there's only one reason left. You are in love?"

"True, oh king," said Roger, drawing hard at his pipe, "I am in love."

"Tell me all about it," said Fanks, curling himself up luxuriously in his chair. "I adore love confidences. When you were a small nuisance at school, you told me all your troubles, and I consoled you. Do so now, and—"

"No! no!" cried Axton, suddenly, "you can't console me now.

27

No one can do that."

"That remains to be seen," said Fanks, smiling. "Come now, Roger, tell me your trouble. Though we have been parted for ten years, I have often thought of my school friend. Unburden your heart to me; it will relieve your mind if it does nothing else."

Thus adjured, Roger brightened up, and settling himself comfortably in his chair, put his feet against the mantelpiece, blew a thick cloud of smoke, and began to tell his story.

"I'm afraid my story hasn't the merit of novelty," he said, candidly. "After you left school I remained, as you know. Then my parents died—within a few months of each other —and I found myself a well-provided orphan. When I say well-provided, I mean that I had an income of three hundred a year, and one can always live comfortably on six pounds a week, if not extravagant. Being thus independent of the world, the flesh, and the devil, meaning thereby the employer, the publisher, and the critic, I went in for writing poetry. It didn't pay, of course, this being the age of sensational literature; but verse manufacturing amused me, and I wandered all over England and the Continent in a desultory sort of way. A kind of grand tour in the poet line, midway between the poverty of Goldsmith and the luxury of Byron. I published a book of poems and the critics abused it—found plenty of faults and no virtues. Well, I was wrathful at this new massacre of the literary innocents and fled to the land of Egypt—in plain English I went down to Ventnor in the Isle of Wight. There I met Her—"

"With a large 'H,' of course," murmured Mr. Fanks, sympathetically.

"For the second time. I then—"

28

"Ah! May I ask where you met her for the first time?"

"Oh, in some other place," said Roger, evasively; "but that's got nothing to do with the subject. The first time we met — well, it was the first time."

"I didn't think it was the second, fond lover. But I understand the second time was the critical one."

"Exactly! It was last August," said Axton, speaking rapidly, so as to give Fanks no further opportunity of interrupting. "I was, as I have stated, at Ventnor, with the idea of writing a drama—Shakespearean, of course—Elizabethan style, you understand, with a dash of modern cynicism, and *fin de siècle* flippancy in it. Wandering about Ventnor, I came across Judith Varlins."

"For the second time of asking—I mean meeting," interpolated Fanks, lightly. "So her name was Judith. Heroic name, suggestive of queenly woman, dark-browed Cleopatra, and all that sort of thing. I picture to myself a grand Semiramis."

Roger shook his head.

"No; she was not a handsome woman. Tall, graceful, dark-browed, if you like, but not pretty."

"Pshaw! who ever called regal Semiramis pretty? Such a weak adjective. But I guess your meaning. Her mind was more beautiful than her face."

"If her face had been as beautiful as her mind, sir," replied Axton, in the Johnsonian style, "she would have been the most beautiful woman in the world."

"Like Dulcinea, eh, Don Quixote Roger? Well; and you met

29

often—juxtaposition is fatal—and love sprang up like Jonah's gourd in one night."

"No; she was not a woman to be lightly won. Judith had with her a cousin—a pretty, golden-haired damsel, whom she worshipped."

"Oh! had you met Golden-hair before?"

"Yes; but I didn't take much notice of her."

"Of course. Preferred brunette to blonde!"

"Decidedly. Well, Florry Marson—"

"The blue-eyed darling?"

"Yes. Florry Marson was a foolish, frivolous little thing, who had been confided to Judith's care by her dead mother."

"Whose dead mother, Florry's or Judith's?" asked Fanks, lightly.

"Florry's, of course," replied Roger, impatiently; "and Judith looked after her like the apple of her eye, though I'm afraid she had rather a hard task, for Miss Marson was one of those irritating girls who did all manner of things without thinking. She was engaged to marry a man called Spolger."

"Anything to do with 'Spolger's Soother, a Good Night's Rest'?"

"Yes; he's the owner."

"Oh! and frivolous Florry didn't like him."

"How do you know?" asked Roger, in a startled tone.

"Because I've seen Spolger's Soother, and he's not pretty

enough for such an empty-headed minx as you describe Miss Marson."

"You are right. She was engaged to him by her father's desire, but she loved a scamp—good-looking, of course, with no money, and had been exiled to Ventnor to escape him."

"Eh! It's quite a romance," said Fanks, gaily. "What was the scamp's name?"

Roger fidgeted in his chair before replying, which action did not escape the lynx eyes of Mr. Fanks, who said nothing, but waited.

"I don't know," said Roger, turning away his head.

"That's a lie," thought Octavius, as he saw the manner in which Mr. Axton replied to a seemingly simple question. "Queer! Why should he tell me such a useless lie?"

"I don't know anything about the scamp," went on Axton, hurriedly; "but he is the cause of all my unhappiness."

"How so?"

"Because Judith—Miss Varlins—refused to marry me on his account."

"What! she loved him also. Fascinating scamp!"

"I don't know if she loved him exactly," said Axton, in a musing tone. "The reason she gave me for her rejection of my proposal was that she could not leave her cousin Florence; but she seemed strangely moved when she spoke of—of Florry's lover."

"Don't you remember his name?" asked Fanks, noticing the

momentary hesitation.

"No, I don't," replied Roger, angrily. "Why do you keep asking me that question?"

"Oh, nothing," said Octavius, quietly; "only I thought that as these two girls had told you so much about themselves, they might have told you more."

"Judith Varlins is a very reserved woman."

"And Miss Marson?"

"I didn't see much of her," answered Roger, moodily, "nor did I wish to—a frivolous little minx, who came between me and my happiness. Well, there's nothing more to tell. After my rejection I left Ventnor for London, and ultimately came down here on a walking tour."

"You've not seen Miss Varlins since, I suppose?"

Again Roger turned away his head, and again the action is noted by Mr. Fanks.

"No," replied Axton, in a low voice. "I—I have not seen her since."

"Lie number two," thought Octavius, wonderingly. "What does it all mean? Do you correspond with her?" he asked, aloud.

"No! Confound it, Fanks, don't put me in the witness-box," cried Roger, rising to his feet.

"I beg your pardon, old fellow," said Octavius, meekly, "it's a habit I've got. A very bad one, I'm afraid. Well, I hope things will go well with you and the marriage with Miss Varlins will take place."

Roger, who was walking rapidly up and down the long room, now vanishing into the chill shadow, anon emerging into the warm lamp-light, stopped at the sound of the name and flung up his arms with a low cry of anguish.

"Never! never!" he cried bitterly, "I shall never marry her."

"Poor old chap, you do seem to be hard hit," said Octavius, sympathetically, "but hope for the best. Florry will marry her patent medicine man, and forget the scamp. Judith will marry you and forget Florry, so things will come out all straight in the long run."

"I hope so," said Axton, resuming his seat, rather ashamed of his emotion; "but they don't look very promising at present. Ah, well, it's no use fighting Destiny. Do you remember the grim view old Sophocles takes of that deity? A classic Juggernaut, crushing all who oppose her. I trust I won't be one of her victims, but I'm doubtful. However, now I've told you my story, what about your own?"

"Mine," said Mr. Fanks, lightly; "bless you, Roger, I'm like Canning's knife-grinder, I've got none to tell. As you know, I'm the eighth son of an impoverished country gentleman, hence my name, Octavius. All my brothers were put into the army, the navy, the Church, and all that sort of thing, so when my turn came to make a *début* in life there was nothing left for me to do. My father, at his wits' end, suggested the colonies, that refuge for destitute younger sons, but I didn't care about turning digger or sheep farmer, and positively refused to be exiled. I came up to London to look round, and made my choice. Being fond of puzzles and cryptograms, I thought I would turn my ingenuity in unravelling enigmas to practical account, and became a detective. The family cast me off; however, I didn't mind that. I left off the name of Rixton and took that of Fanks—

my old school name, you remember — so I didn't disgrace the Rixtons of Derbyshire. Being a gentleman doesn't mean bread and butter in these democratic days; and though my pedigree's as long as the tail of a kite, it was quite as useless in a commercial sense. Besides, the detective business is just as honourable as any other, and also very exciting, so I don't regret having gone in for it. I get well paid also, and the life suits me."

"Is your father reconciled to you yet?"

"Oh, yes, in a sort of a way; but the Vidocq business sticks in his throat and he can't swallow it. However, I visit the paternal acres sometimes, and no one thinks Octavius Rixton, gentleman, has anything to do with Octavius Fanks, detective."

"And you like your profession?"

"I adore it. Mystery has a wonderful charm for human nature, and there's a marvellous fascination in joining together a criminal puzzle. I've had all kinds of queer cases through my hands dealing with the seamy side of humanity, and have been uniformly successful with the lot. This affair, however, puzzles me dreadfully."

"It's a horrible thing," said Roger, relighting his pipe, which had gone out. "I went for a long walk to-day so as to avoid the inquest."

"Ah, you poets have not got strong nerves."

"I'm afraid not. I hear the verdict was suicide."

"Yes, and I don't agree with the verdict."

Roger turned round quickly, and looked straight at his

companion, who was staring absently at the fire.

"Indeed," he said at length. "Why not?"

"Eh! Oh, I don't know; I've got my reasons," replied Fanks, coolly, evidently not wishing to continue the subject. "By the way, how long are you going to stop here?"

"Just for to-night; I'm off to-morrow."

"So am I. London?"

"No, I'm going to continue my walking tour."

"Ah, sly dog," cried Fanks, gaily, "I understand. You are going to look up Miss Varlins again."

Roger bit his nether lip hard, and replied, coldly, in a somewhat sober fashion, neither affirming nor denying the insinuation:

"I won't find her down here at all events."

"Oh! Then she's still at Ventnor?"

"No! She and Miss Marson have gone home."

"Really! And where is home?"

"My dear Fanks, your cross-examination is most trying."

"I beg your pardon," said Octavius, ceremoniously, "I was not aware I had asked an impertinent question."

"Nor have you, my dear fellow," cried Axton, cordially. "Don't mind my bad temper, I can't help it. My nerves are all unstrung with this horrible business of the inquest. There's no reason why I should not tell you where Miss Varlins lives."

"Oh, never mind," said Fanks, a trifle coldly; "I don't want to know."

"Don't get offended at nothing, Octavius," replied Roger, in an injured tone; "I will tell you if it's only to make amends for my rudeness. Miss Varlins lives at Ironfields."

The detective jumped to his feet with a sudden ejaculation, at which Axton also arose, looking pale and alarmed.

"What's the matter, Fanks?" he asked, hurriedly.

For answer, Octavius Fanks drew the pill-box from his pocket, and placing it silently on the table, pointed to the inscription on the lid:

"Wosk & Co.
Chemists, Ironfields."

Chapter 3

Purely Theoretical

Roger Axton stood looking at the pill-box on the table, and Octavius Fanks stood looking at Roger Axton, the former lost in a fit of painful musing (evident from his pale face, his twitching lips, his startled expression), the latter keenly observant, according to his usual habits. At last Roger with a deep sigh drew his hand across his brow and resumed his seat, while Mr. Fanks, picking up the pill-box, gave it a cheerful rattle as he followed his example.

"What a strange coincidence," he said, thoughtfully; "but I'm not astonished. This sort of thing occurs in real life as well as in novels. 'Truth is stranger than fiction.' I don't know who first made that remark, but he was a wise man, you may depend, and wonderfully observant of events before he crystallised his experience in those five words."

"It certainly is curious," replied Roger, absently, as though he were thinking of something else. "Fancy finding the name of the town where She—"

"With a large S, of course."

"Where she lives, printed on a pill-box," finished Roger, and then, after a pause: "What do you think of it, Fanks?"

"Think!" repeated Octavius, thoughtfully. "Oh, I think it is the clue to the whole mystery."

"Why, what do you mean?" asked Roger, in a startled tone.

"What I say," retorted Fanks, twirling the pill-box round and round. "It's not difficult of comprehension. Man, name unknown, comes down here, and dies shortly after his arrival. Inquest; verdict, suicide! Fiddle-de-dee! Murder! And this pill-box is the first link in the chain that will bind the criminal. By the way," said Octavius, suddenly struck with a new idea, "how long have you been at Jarlchester?"

"A week."

"Oh! Then you were here when the man died?"

"I was."

"Humph! Excuse my witness-box manner!"

"Don't apologise," said Roger, quietly. "Cross-examine me as much as you like. It seems second nature with detectives to suspect every one."

"Suspect!" repeated Octavius, in an injured tone. "Good heavens, Axton, what are you talking about? I'd as soon think of suspecting myself, you peppery young ass. But I'm anxious to find out all about this affair, and naturally ask the people who lived under the same roof as the dead man. You are one of the people, so I ask you."

"Ask me what?"

"Oh, several things."

"Well, go on; but I warn you I know nothing," said Roger, gloomily.

"I tell you what, young man," observed Mr. Fanks, sententiously, "you need shaking up a bit. This love affair has made you view all things in a most bilious fashion. An overdose of love, and poetry, and solitude incapacitates a human being for enjoying life, so if you are wise—which I beg leave to doubt—you will brace up your nerves by helping me to find out this mystery."

"I'm afraid I'd make a sorry detective, Octavius."

"That remains to be proved. See here, old boy. I was called down here about this case, and as the wiseacres of Jarlchester have settled it to their own satisfaction that there is—to their minds—no more need for my services, I am discharged—dismissed—turned out by Jarlchester & Co.; but as I don't often get such a clever case to look after, I'm going to find out the whole affair for my own pleasure."

"It seems a disease with you, this insatiable curiosity to find out things."

"Ay, that it is. We call it detective fever. Join me in this case, and you'll find yourself suffering from the disease in a wonderfully short space of time."

"No, thank you; I prefer my freedom."

"And your idleness! Well, go your own way, Roger. If you won't take the medicine I prescribe, you certainly won't be cured. Unrequited love will lie heavy on your heart, and your health and work will suffer in consequence. Both will be dull, and between doctors and critics you will have a high old time of it, dear boy."

"What nonsense you do talk!" said Roger, fretfully.

"Eh! do you think so? Perhaps I'm like Touchstone, and use my folly as a stalking-horse behind which to shoot my wit. I'm not sure if I'm quoting rightly, but the moral is apparent. However, all this is not to the point—to my point, I mean—and if you have not got detective fever I have, so I will use you as a medicine to allay the disease."

"Fire away, old fellow," said Axton, turning his chair half round so as to place his tell-tale face in the shadow, thereby rendering it undecipherable to Fanks; "I'm all attention."

Octavius at once produced his secretive little note-book and vicious little pencil, which latter assumed dramatic significance in the nervous fingers that held it.

"I'm ready," said Fanks, letting his pencil-point jest on a clean white page. "Question first: Did you know this dead man?"

"Good heavens, no. I don't even know his name nor his appearance."

"You have never seen him?"

"How could I have seen him? I am exploring the neighbourhood, and generally start on my travels in the morning early and return late. This man arrived at five, went to bed at nine, and as I didn't come back till ten o'clock I didn't see him on that night; next morning he was dead."

"Did you not see the corpse?"

"No," said Roger, with a shudder, "I don't care for such 'wormy circumstance.'"

"Wormy circumstance is good," remarked Fanks, approvingly. "Keats, I think. Yes, I thought so. I see you don't care for horrors. You are not of the Poe-Baudelaire school of grave-digging, corpse-craving poesy."

"Hardly! I don't believe in going to the gutter for inspiration."

"Ah! now you are thinking of MM. Zola and Gondrecourt, my friend; but, dear me, how one thing does lead to another. We are discussing literature instead of murder. Let us return to our first loves. Why didn't you attend the inquest?"

"Because I didn't want to."

"An all-sufficient reason, indeed," remarked Mr. Fanks, drily, making digs at his book with the pencil. "I wonder you weren't called as a witness."

"No necessity. I know nothing of the affair."

"Absolutely nothing?" (interrogative).

"Absolutely nothing." (decisive).

Mr. Fanks twirled his vicious little pencil in his fingers, closed his secretive little book with a snap, and replaced them both in his pocket with a sigh.

"You are a most unsatisfactory medicine, my dear Roger. You have done nothing to cure my detective fever."

"Am I so bad as that? Come now, I'll tell you one thing: I slept in the room next to that of the dead man."

"You did?"

"Yes."

"And you heard nothing on that night!"

"If you walked twenty miles during the day, Fanks, you would have been too tired to listen for the sounds of a possible murder."

"Yes, yes, of course. What a pity we can't look twenty-four hours ahead of things; it would save such a lot of trouble."

"And prevent such a lot of murders. If such prophetic power were given to humanity, I'm afraid your occupation would be gone."

"Othello's remark! yes, of course; but I'm sorry you slept so soundly on that night, as some one might have been in the dead man's room."

"Why do you think so?" asked Roger, quickly.

"Because the door was slightly ajar," replied Fanks, sagaciously; "a nervous man would not have slept with his door like that. You're sure you heard nothing?"

"Quite sure."

"It's a pity—a great pity. By the way, have you ever been to Ironfields?"

Roger hesitated, turned uneasily in his chair, and at last blurted out:

"No; I have never been to Ironfields."

"Humph!" said Fanks, looking doubtfully at him. "I thought you might have met Miss Varlins there for the first time."

"So I might," replied Roger, equably; "at the same time I might have met her in London."

"So you don't know anything about Ironfields."

"Only that it is a manufacturing town given over to the domination of foundries and millionaires in the iron interest; to me it is simply a geographical expression."

"I plead guilty to the same state of ignorance, but I will shortly be wiser, because I am going down to Ironfields."

"What for?" demanded Roger, with a start.

"I shouldn't let you into the secrets of the prison house," said Mr. Fanks, severely; "but as you are 'mine own familiar friend'—Shakespeare again, ubiquitous poet well, as you are mine own familiar friend, I don't mind telling you in confidence, I'm going down to see Wosk & Co., of Ironfields, Chemists."

"And your object?"

"Is to find out the name of the gentleman who bought those pills."

"I don't see what good that will do."

"Blind, quite blind," said Octavius, nodding his head mournfully. "I will unfold myself—the immortal bard for the third time. When I find out the name of the deceased, which I can do through that pill-box, I will be able to find out all about his antecedents. Satisfied on that point, it is possible, nay probable, that I may find some one who has ill-feelings towards him."

"And therefore poisons him in Jarlchester while they remain at Ironfields," said Roger, ironically. "I congratulate you on your clear-sightedness."

"It's puzzling, certainly, very puzzling," replied Fanks, rubbing his head with an air of vexation. "I've got absolutely nothing to work on."

"And are going to work on it. Pish! sandy foundations."

"Now look here, Roger," cried the detective, with great energy, "let us survey this case from a common-sense point of view. This man couldn't have come down to Jarlchester to commit suicide; he could have done that at Ironfields."

"Perhaps he wanted to spare his friends—if he had any—the pain of knowing that he died by his own hand."

"Rubbish! Suicides are not so considerate, as a rule. They generally make away with themselves in a most public manner, so as to draw attention to their wrongs. No, I can't and won't believe that this man, who gave no hint of wishing to die, came down here to do so."

"Then if he did not kill himself, who did?"

"Ah, that's what I've got to find out."

"Yes, and what if you don't find out."

"Perhaps yes, perhaps no. Murder will out. Clever remark that. But to continue: I always look on both sides of the question. It may be a case of suicide."

"It is a case of suicide. I believe the jury are right," said Roger, firmly.

"You seem very certain about it," remarked Fanks, a trifle annoyed.

"I only judge from what I have heard."

"Rumour, mere rumour."

"Not at all. Facts, my friend, facts. I allude to the evidence at the inquest."

Octavius made no reply at first, but jumping up from his chair, began to walk to and fro with a frown on his face.

"I dare say you're right," he said, at length; "taking the evidence as a whole, I suppose the jury could only bring in a verdict of suicide. No one could have poisoned him. No one here knew him, therefore had no reason to get rid of him. He took that morphia, opium, or whatever it was, sure enough, and I firmly believe of his own free will. Judging from that theory, it looks decidedly like suicide; but then, again, he may have taken the morphia, not knowing it was poison. It could not have been the pills, for they only contain arsenic. He might certainly have taken morphia in order to get to sleep, as from all accounts he suffered from insomnia—nerves, I suppose. But then some portion of what he took would have been found, and if not that, then the bottle that held the drug or sleeping draught; but nothing was found, absolutely nothing. He is discovered dead from an overdose of morphia, and no traces of morphia —bottle or otherwise—are found in his room. If it was suicide, he would not have taken such precautions, seeing he had nothing to gain by concealing the mode of his death. If it was murder, some one must have administered it to him under the guise of a harmless drug; but then no one here knew him, so no one could have done so. You see, therefore, my dear Roger, from this statement of the case, that I am absolutely at a stand still."

"Yes, I think you can do nothing, so your best plan is to accept the verdict of suicide, and forget all about it."

"And this pill-box?"

"Well, you gain nothing from that except the name of the

place where the dead man bought it. If you go to the chemist you will find out his name, certainly."

"And the circumstances of his life also. You forget that."

"No, I don't. But such discovery will hardly account for his murder here. If you find out from your inquiries at Ironfields that the dead man had an enemy, you will have to prove how that enemy came down here and secretly poisoned him. Judging from all the evidence, there is no trace of poison left behind, no one has been staying in this inn except myself, so I really don't see how you are going to bring the crime home to any particular person."

Having finished this speech, Roger arose to his feet with a yawn, and knocked the ashes out of his pipe against the mantelpiece.

"Where are you going?" asked Fanks, stopping in his walk.

"To bed, of course. I've had a long day."

"You continue your walking tour to-morrow?"

"Yes. I start at ten o'clock. And you?"

"I am going down to Ironfields."

"On a wild-goose chase."

"That remains to be proved," retorted Fanks, grimly.

"I'm certain of it, so your wisest plan is to accept the inevitable and give this case up," replied Axton, holding out his hand. "Good night."

"Good night, old boy," said Octavius, cordially. "I'm very pleased to meet you again. By the way, don't let us lose sight of one another. My address is Scotland Yard—my Fanks address, of course. And yours?"

"Temple Chambers, Fleet Street."

Out came Mr. Fanks' secretive little note-book, in which, he wrote down the address with a gay laugh.

"Ha! ha! Like all literary men, you start with the law and leave it for the profits."

"Of poetry. Pshaw!"

"Eh, who knows? Every scribbler carries the Laureate-ship in his brain. By the way, if I see Miss Varlins at Ironfields, shall I give her any message?"

"No; she won't have anything to do with me," replied Roger, dismally. "I've no doubt I'll get married some day, but it won't be to Judith Varlins."

"Ardent lover!" said Fanks, laughing. "Well, good night, and pleasant dreams."

"With that body upstairs. Ugh!" cried Roger Axton, and vanished with a shudder.

Mr. Fanks stood beside the dying fire, leaning his two elbows on the mantelpiece, and thinking deeply.

"He's very much altered," he thought, drearily. "Not the bright boy of ten years ago. How trouble does change a man, and love also! I'll make a point of seeing Miss Varlins when I go down to Ironfields. Rather a dismal love story, but what the devil did he tell me two lies for?"

He left the room, took his candle from Miss Chickles, and returned to bed. As he closed the door of his room, his thoughts reverted to Roger Axton once more.

"He told me two deliberate lies," he thought, with a puzzled expression on his face. "I could see that by his face, or, rather, his manner. Humph! I don't like this."

Having placed the candle on the dressing-table, Mr. Fanks sat down, and having produced his secretive note-book, proceeded to make therein a memorandum (in shorthand) of his conversation with Axton.

No reason for doing so; certainly not. Still, name on pill-box, Ironfields; residence of Judith Varlins, Ironfields. Curious coincidence—very. Nothing may come of it. Highly improbable anything could come of it. Still, those few lines of queer signs, recording an unimportant conversation, may be of use in the future. Who knows? Ah, who, indeed? There's a good deal in chance, and fate sometimes puts a thread into our hands which conducts through tangled labyrinths to unknown issues.

"Two lies," said Mr. Fanks for the third time, as he rolled himself up in the bed-clothes and blew out the candle. "He hadn't seen her since Ventnor. He hadn't heard from her since Ventnor. Wonderful self-denial for a young man in love. I'd like to know more about Roger's little romance."

Extracts from a Detective's Note-Book

"Can't make Axton out . . . Most curious conversation— inquisitive on my part, evasive on his . . . He told me two lies . . . In fact, during the whole conversation he seemed to

48

be on his guard. . . . I don't like the look of things . . . I have no right to pry into Axton's affairs, but I can't understand his denials—denials which I could tell from his manner were false . . . Queer thing about Ironfields . . . The dead man came from Ironfields . . . Miss Varlins lives at Ironfields . . . Qy. Can there be any connection between the deceased and Miss Varlins? . . . Impossible, and yet it's very strange . . . I don't like that open door either . . . That is extraordinary . . . Then the letter written by the deceased . . . I asked at the post office here about it . . . They could tell me nothing . . . I wonder to whom that letter was sent? . . . I think it's the key to the whole affair . . . Can Roger Axton be keeping anything from me? . . . Did he know the dead man? . . . I am afraid to answer these questions . . . Well, I'll go down to Ironfields and find out all about the dead man . . . Perhaps my inquiries will lead me to Miss Varlins . . . But no, there can be no connection, and yet I doubt Roger . . . I mistrust him . . . I don't like his manner . . . his evasive replies . . . And then he's connected with Miss Varlins—she is connected with Ironfields . . . That is connected with the deceased . . . All links in a chain . . . Most extraordinary.

"*Mem.*—To go at once to Ironfields."

Chapter 4

The Evidence of the Chemist's Assistant

Ironfields is not a pretty place; not even its warmest admirer could say it was pretty, but then its warmest admirer would not want to say anything of the kind. Well drained, well laid out, well lighted, it could—according to the minds of its inhabitants—easily dispense with such mere prettiness or picturesqueness as crooked-streeted, gable-mansioned towns, dating from the Middle Ages, could boast of. Poor things, those sleepy cathedral towns, beautified by the hand of Time—poor things indeed compared with vast Ironfields, the outcome of a manufacturing century and a utilitarian race! Ironfields with its lines of ugly model houses, its broad, treeless streets, its muddy river flowing under a hideous railway bridge, its mighty foundries with their tall chimneys that belched forth smoke in the daytime, and fire at night, and its ceaseless clamour that roared up to the smoke-hidden sky six days in the week.

The inhabitants were a race of Cyclops. Rough, swarthy men of herculean build, scant of speech and of courtesy, worn-looking women, with vinegary faces peering sharply at every one from under the shawls they wore on their tousled heads, and tribes of squalling brats, with just enough clothes for decency, grimy with the smoky, sooty atmosphere, looking like legions of small devils as they played in the barren streets, piercing the deafening clamour with their shrill, unchildlike voices. A manufacturing town, inhabited by humanity with no idea of beauty, with no desire beyond an increase of weekly wage, or an extra drink at the public-house. Humanity with a hard, unlovely religion expounded in hideous little chapels by fervid preachers of severe principles. A glorious triumph of our highest civilisation, this matter-of-fact city, with its creed of work, work, work, and its eyes constantly on the sordid things of this earth, and never raised to the blue sky of heaven. A glorious triumph indeed—for the capitalists.

When it rained—which it did frequently—Ironfields was sloppy, and when Ironfields was sloppy it was detestable; for the rain coming down through the smoky cloud that constantly lowered over the town, made everything, if possible, more grimy than before. But Ironfields was quite content; it was a name of note in commercial circles, and its products went forth to the four quarters of the world, bringing back in exchange plenty of money, of which a great deal found its way into the pockets of the master, and very little into those of the man.

The country around was not pretty. Nature, with that black, ugly, clamorous city constantly before her eyes, lost heart in her work, and did not attempt to place beauties before the eyes of people who did not know anything about beauty, and would have thought it a very useless thing if they had. So the fields lying round Ironfields were only a shade better than the city itself, for the shadow of smoke lay over everything, and where sunshine is not, cheerfulness is wanting.

On one side of Ironfields, however, Nature had made a feeble attempt to assert herself, but then it was in a queer little village which had been the germ from whence arose this noisy town. In the old days the queer little village had stood amid green fields beside a sparkling river; but now the fields had disappeared, the sparkling river had turned to a dull, muddy stream, and the little village was improved out of all recognition. Like Frankenstein, it had created a monster which dominated it entirely, which took away even its name and reduced it from a quaint, pretty place, redolent of pastoral joys, to a dull little suburb, mostly inhabited by poor people. True, beyond stood the mansions of the Ironfields millionaires, glaring and unpicturesque, in equally glaring gardens laid out with mathematical accuracy; but the upper ten merely drove through the village on their way to these Brummagem palaces, and did not acknowledge its existence in any way. Yet a good many of their progenitors had lived in the dull suburb before Ironfields was Ironfields, but they forgot all about that in the enjoyment of their new-found splendours, and the miserable village was now a kind of poor relation, unrecognised, uncared for, and very much despised.

In the principal street, narrow and winding, with old houses on either side, standing like dismal ghosts of the past, was the chemist's shop, a brand-new place, with plate-glass windows, and the name, "Wosk & Co.," in bright gold letters on a bright blue ground. Behind the plate-glass windows appeared huge bottles containing liquids red, and yellow, and green in colour, which threw demoniacal reflections on the faces of passers-by at night, when the gas flared behind them. All kinds of patent medicines were there displayed to the best advantage; bottles of tooth-brushes, cakes of Pears' soap, phials of queer shape and wondrous virtue, sponges, jars of leeches, queer-looking pipes compounded of glass and india-rubber tubing, packets of fly-exterminators, and various other strange things pertaining to the trade, all calling attention to their various excellencies in neat little printed leaflets scattered promiscuously throughout.

Within, a shining counter of mahogany laden with cures for the various ills which flesh is heir to; and at the far end, a neat little glass screen with a gas-jet on top, above which could be seen the gray-black head of Mr. Wosk and the smooth red head of Mr. Wosk's assistant.

Mr. Wosk (who was also the Co.) was a slender, serious man, always clothed in black, with a sedate, black-bearded countenance, a habit of washing his hands with invisible

52

soap and water, and a rasping little cough, which he introduced into his conversation at inopportune moments. He would have made an excellent undertaker, an ideal mute, for his cast of countenance was undeniably mournful, but Fate had fitted this round peg of an undertaker into the square hole of a chemist in a fit of perverse anger. He bore up, however, against his uncongenial situation with dreary resignation, and dispensed his own medicines with an air of saying, "I hope it will do you good, but I'm afraid it won't." He was the pillar of the Church in a small way, and stole round the chapel on Sundays with the plate in a melancholy fashion, as if he was asking some good Christian to put some food on the plate and despaired of getting it. Ebenezer was his name, and his wife, an acidulated lady of uncertain age, ruled him with a rod of iron, perhaps from the fact that she had no children over whom to domineer.

Mrs. Wosk, however, could not rule the assistant, much as she desired to do so. Not that he made any show of opposition, but always twisted this way and turned that in an eel-like fashion until she did not know quite where to have him. In fact, the assistant ruled Mrs. Wosk (of which rule she had a kind of uneasy consciousness), and as Mrs. Wosk ruled Mr. Wosk, including the Co., M. Jules Guinaud may have been said to have ruled the whole household.

A hard name to pronounce, especially in Ironfields, where French was in the main an unknown tongue, so suburban Ironfields, by common consent, forgot the surname of the assistant, and called him, in friendly fashion, Munseer Joolees, by which appellation he was known for a considerable time. Mrs. Wosk, however, who meddled a good deal with the shop and saw a good deal of the assistant, being learned in Biblical lore (as the wife of a deacon should be), found a certain resemblance suggested by the name and appearance of the assistant between Munseer Joolees and Judas Iscariot, whereupon, with virulent wit, she christened him by the latter name, and Monsieur Joolees became widely known as Monsieur Judas, which name pleased the Ironfields worthies, being easy to pronounce and containing a certain epigrammatic flavour.

The name suited him, too, this slender, undersized man with the stealthy step of a cat; the unsteady greenish eyes that appeared to see nothing, yet took in everything; the smooth, shining red hair plastered tightly down on his egg-shaped skull; and the delicate, pink and white-complexioned, hairless face that bore the impress of a kind of evil beauty—yes, the name suited him admirably, and as he took no exception to it, being in suburban Ironfields opinion an atheist, and therefore ignorant of the Biblical significance of the title, nobody thought of addressing him by any other.

He spoke English moderately well, in a soft, sibilant voice with a foreign accent, and sometimes used French words, which were Greek to all around him. Expressive, too, in a pantomimic way, with his habit of shrugging his sloping shoulders, his method of waving his slim white hands when in conversation, and a certain talent in using his eyes to convey his meaning. Lids drooping downwards, "I listen humbly to your words of wisdom, monsieur." Suddenly raising them so as to display full optic, "Yes, you may look at me; I am a most guileless person." Narrowing to a mere slit, like the pupil of a cat's eye, "Beware, I am dangerous," and so forth, all of which, in conjunction with the aforesaid shrugs and pantomimic action of his hands, made the conversation of Monsieur Judas very intelligible indeed, in spite of his foreign accent and French observations.

It was raining on this particular morning—seasonable weather, of course; but as far as rain went, all the months were the same in Ironfields, and a thick, black fog pervaded the atmosphere. A cold, clammy fog, with a sooty flavour, that crept slowly through the streets and into the houses, like a wounded snake dragging itself along. Here and there pedestrians looming large in the opaque cloud like gigantic apparitions, gas-lamps flaring drearily in the thick air, cabs and carts and carriages all moving cautiously along like endless funerals. And only two o'clock in the afternoon. Surely the darkness which spread over the land of Egypt could be no worse than this; nay, perhaps it was better, Egypt being tropical and lacking the chill, unwholesome moisture which permeated the air, wrapping the dingy houses, the noisy foundries, and the cheerless streets in a dull, sodden pall.

Gas glared in the shop of Wosk & Co., behind the glass doors, which kept out as much of the fog as they were able —gas which gave forth a dim, yellow light to Mr. Wosk behind the screen, looking over prescriptions, and to Monsieur Judas at the counter making up neat packages of medicine bottles. At the little window at the back which looked into the Wosk dwelling-house, an occasional vision of Mrs. Wosk's head appeared like that of a cross cherub, keeping her eye on chemist and assistant.

"Bur-r-r," says Monsieur Judas, blowing on his lean fingers, "it is to me the most coldness of times. Aha! le brouillard! it makes itself to be all the places to-day."

"Seasonable, seasonable!" murmurs Mr. Wosk, washing his hands in a contemplative fashion. "Good for—ahem!—good for business—that is, business in our line—ahem!"

"Eh, Monsieur Vosks! mais oui, mon ami," answered the

Frenchman, raising his eyebrows, "and for de—what you call de coffins man. L'homme des funerailles."

"That, ahem!" said Mr. Wosk, with his rasping cough, "is what we must try and prevent. The undertaker—not coffins man, Monsieur Judas, that is not—ahem—correct Anglo-Saxon—is the last, the very last resource of a sick man. Prevention—ahem—in the person of ourselves is better than —ahem—dear me—I don't think the remark is app—ahem—applicable."

At this moment the glass doors opened to admit a stranger, enveloped in a comfortable fur coat, and also gave admission to a cloud of fog that had been waiting for the opportunity for some time. The stranger made his appearance like a Homeric deity, in a cloudy fashion, and when the attendant fog dispersed, Monsieur Judas (inquisitive) and Mr. Wosk (mournfully indifferent) saw that he was a keen-faced young gentleman with a sharp, decisive manner.

"Wosk & Co., eh!" queried the stranger, who was none other than Mr. Octavius Fanks.

"Yes, sir," said Mr. Wosk, advancing, "the name—ahem—my name, sir, is in front of the—the shop, sir."

"So is the fog," replied the detective, drily, leaning over the counter. "I could hardly see the shop, much less the name."

"De fog is still heavier, monsieur?" said Judas, taking in the appearance of Mr. Fanks in a comprehensive fashion.

Octavius swung sharply round at the sound of the foreign voice, and instantly took an intuitive dislike to the appearance of the red-haired young man.

"Oui," he replied, looking at him sharply; "n'êtes-vous pas

Français?"

"Monsieur a beaucoup de pénétration," said Judas, startled at hearing his own tongue.

His eyes had narrowed into those dangerous slits which betokened that he was on his guard against this clever—too clever Englishman. The two men looked at one another steadily for a moment, and two ideas flashed rapidly through their respective minds.

The Fanks idea, suggested by the suspicious appearance (to a detective) of Monsieur Judas:

"This man has a past, and is always on his guard."

The Guinaud idea, inspired by a naturally suspicious nature:

"This Englishman is a possible enemy. I must be careful."

There was really no ground for such uncomplimentary ideas on the part of these two men who now met for the first time, except that instinctive repulsion which springs from the collision of two natures antipathetic to one another.

Mr. Wosk, being warned by the apparition of Mrs. Wosk's head at the little window that he was wasting time, addressed himself at once to his customer in a business fashion:

"What can I do for you, sir?"

Octavius withdrew his eyes from the face of the assistant, and producing a pill-box, laid it down on the counter before Mr. Wosk.

"I want to know the name of the gentleman for whom you

made up these pills."

"Rather difficult to say, sir," said Mr. Wosk, taking up the box; "we make up so many boxes like this."

"They were made up for a gentleman who left Ironfields shortly afterwards."

The chemist, never very clear-headed at any time, looked perfectly bewildered at being called upon to make such a sudden explanation, and turned helplessly to his assistant, who stood working at his medicine bottles with downcast eyes.

"I'm afraid—ahem—really, my memory is so bad," he faltered, childishly; "well, I scarcely—ahem—but I think Monsieur Judas will be able to tell you all about it. I have the—ahem—I have the fullest confidence in Monsieur Judas."

"It's more than I should have," thought Fanks, as the assistant silently took the pill-box from his master and opened it.

"Eight pilules," he said, counting them.

"Yes, eight pills," replied Fanks, taking a seat by the counter, "but, of course, when you made up the prescription there must have been more."

"De monsieur weeth de pilules did he geeve dem to monsieur?"

"No; I want to know the gentleman's name."

"An' for wy, monsieur?"

"Never you mind," retorted Octavius, coolly; "you do what

you're asked, my good fellow."

The "good fellow" gave Mr. Fanks an ugly look; but in another moment was bland and smiling as ever. Mr. Wosk (beckoned by the cherub's head) had gone into the back premises, so the two men were quite alone, of which circumstance Mr. Fanks took advantage by speaking to Monsieur Judas in French, in order to understand him better.

Translated, the conversation (guarded on both sides by mutual suspicion) was as follows:

"Will monsieur permit me to ask him a few questions? Otherwise," said Judas, with a shrug, "I cannot hope to find the name monsieur requires."

"Ask whatever questions you like."

"Does monsieur know when the gentleman left this town?"

Mr. Fanks made a rapid calculation, and answered promptly: "I'm not quite sure; after the 6th and before the 13th of the present month. But your best plan will be to go back from the 13th of November."

"Certainly, monsieur."

Judas disappeared behind the neat screen, and rapidly turned up the order book beginning with the 13th of November, as directed.

"They are tonic pills, I see, monsieur," he called out.

"Yes, it is marked on the box."

In another moment Fanks heard an exclamation of surprise behind the screen, and shortly afterwards Monsieur Judas emerged, carrying the order book with him. He was visibly agitated, and his lean hands trembled as he placed the book on the counter.

"What is the matter?" asked Fanks, suspiciously, rising to his feet.

"I will explain to monsieur later on," said Judas, with a sickly smile. "At present, however, here is what you want. These pills were made up for Monsieur Sebastian Melstane."

"Sebastian Melstane," muttered Fanks, thoughtfully. "Oh, that was his name."

"Yes, Sebastian Melstane," said Judas, slowly. "He bought these pills on the 11th of November, and went down to Jarlchester the next day."

"How do you know he went to Jarlchester?" asked Fanks, considerably startled.

"Because I know Sebastian Melstane, monsieur. We lodged at the same pension. He makes me the confidence that he was going to that place, and, I believe, took these pills with him. Now you have the box, but my friend, where is he?"

Monsieur Judas threw out his hands with a fine dramatic gesture, and fixed his crafty eyes on the impassive face of the detective.

"Do you read the papers?" asked Octavius, with great deliberation.

"Yes; but I read English so bad."

"Get some one to translate for you, then," said Fanks, coolly, "and you will see that an unknown man committed suicide at Jarlchester. That man was Sebastian Melstane."

"Gave himself the death?"

"Yes; read the papers. By the way, Monsieur Judas that is your name, I believe—as you knew Sebastian Melstane, I may want to ask you some questions about him."

Monsieur Judas pulled out a card with some writing on it and handed it to Fanks with a flourish.

"My name, monsieur—my habitation, monsieur! If monsieur will do me the honour to call at my pension, I will tell him whatever he desires to know."

"Humph! I'm afraid that's beyond your power, M. Guinaud," replied Fanks, glancing at the card. "However, I'll call round this evening at eight o'clock; but at present I want to know about these pills."

"They were bought by my friend on the 11th," said Judas, showing the entry. "Behold, monsieur, the book speaks it."

"Who signed the prescription?"

"A doctor, monsieur, a doctor. I cannot say the name, it is hard for my tongue; but, monsieur"—struck with a sudden idea—"you shall see his own writing."

Once more he vanished behind the screen, and shortly afterwards reappeared with a sheet of note-paper, which he placed before Octavius.

"There it is, monsieur."

Fanks took up the paper, and read as follows:

R. Acid. Arsen. gi.
Pulv. Glycyrrh. gr. xv.
Ext. Glycyrrh. gr. xxx.
Misce et divide in pilule.
No. XII.
Sig. Tonic pills.
One to be taken before retiring nightly.
Jacob Japix, M.D.

"I see you made up twelve pills," said Fanks, after he had perused this document.

"Yes, monsieur, twelve pills. It is the usual number." Octavius looked thoughtful for a moment, then, turning his back on the assistant, walked to the door, where he stood gazing out at the fog, and thinking deeply in this fashion: "There were twelve pills in the box when Melstane bought it on the 11th of this month. According to his statement to Miss Chickles he took a tonic pill regularly every night. On the 11th, therefore, he took one. Left Ironfields on the 12th, and must have slept in London, as the journey is so long. There he took another pill; and at Jarlchester, on the 13th, he took a third. Dr. Drewey analysed three pills, so that's six accounted for out of the twelve. Exactly half, so there ought only to be six left. But there are eight in the box now. Good Heavens! what is the meaning of those two extra pills?"

Turning sharply round, he walked back to the counter.

"Are you sure you are not making a mistake?" he said, quickly; "you must have made up fourteen pills."

"But, monsieur, behold!" said Judas, pointing to the prescription, "No. XII."

"Yes, that's twelve, sure enough," observed Fanks, trying to appear calm, but feeling excited at the thought that he had stumbled on some tangible evidence at last.

"Did you make up the pills?"

"Yes, I myself, monsieur."

"And you are sure you only made up twelve?"

"On my word of honour, monsieur," said Judas, opening his eyes with their guileless look; "but I do not ask monsieur to believe me if he has doubt. Eh, my faith, no! Monsieur my master also counted the pills."

"That is the custom, I believe," said Mr. Fanks, thoughtfully, "a kind of check."

"But certainly, monsieur, without doubt."

At this moment, as if he knew his presence was required, Mr. Wosk walked into the shop, whereupon Monsieur Judas at once explained the matter to him.

"My assistant is—ahem—correct," said Mr. Wosk, sadly, as if he rather regretted it than otherwise. "I remember Mr. Melstane's tonic pills, and I—ahem—did count them. There were—ahem—twelve."

"You are sure?"

"I am certain."

"An' I to myself can assure it," remarked Judas, in English; "but if monsieur would make to himself visits at monsieur le docteur, he could know exactly of the numbers. Eh bien. Je le crois."

"Where does Dr. Japix live?" asked Fanks, picking up the

pill-box and putting it in his pocket. "I will call round and see him."

Mr. Wosk wrote out the address and handed it to the detective with a bow.

"There's nothing wrong with the—ahem—medicine, I trust," he said, nervously. "I am—ahem—most careful, and my assistant, Monsieur Judas, is much to be—ahem—trusted."

"I don't know if anything's wrong with these pills," said Octavius, touching his breast coat-pocket, "but you know the saying, 'There is more in this than meets the eye.' Shakespeare, you observe. Wonderful man—appropriate remark for everything. Monsieur Guinaud, I will see you to-night. Mr. Wosk, to-morrow expect me about these pills. Good afternoon."

When he had vanished into the fog, which he did as soon as he went outside, Mr. Wosk turned to his assistant with some alarm.

"I trust, Monsieur Judas, that the pills—the pills—"

"They are in themselves qui' right. Eh! oh, yes," replied Monsieur Judas, letting his eyelids droop over his eyes. "To-morrow I to you will speke of dis—dis—eh! le mystère—vous savez, monsieur. Le Mystère Jarlcesterre."

"That thing in the paper," cried Mr. Wosk, aghast. "Why—ahem—what has it got to do—ahem—with us?"

Monsieur Judas shrugged his shoulders, spread out his hands with a deprecating gesture, and spoke slowly:

"Eh, le voila! I myself am no good to rread les journaux

anglais—les feuilletons. If you so kine vil be to me, monsieur, an' rread de Mystère Jarleesterre, I vil to you explin moch, eh! Il est bien entendu."

"But what has the Jarlchester Mystery got to do with us?" repeated Mr. Wosk, helplessly, like a large child.

"Eh, mon ami, qui sait?" replied Monsieur Judas, enraged at his master's stupidity. "De man dead is he who took ze pilules."

"Sebastian Melstane!" cried Mr. Wosk, thunder-struck.

"Oui, c'est le nom!"

And Monsieur Judas narrowed his eyes, spread out his lean hands, and smiled complacently at the look of horror on the face of Mr. Wosk.

Chapter 5

Dr. Japix Speaks

Octavius Fanks had no difficulty in finding the residence of Dr. Jacob Japix, for that kind-hearted gentleman was well known in Ironfields, not alone in the village suburb, but throughout the great city itself, where his beaming face, his cheery words, and his open hand were much appreciated, especially in the quarters of the poor. Not a professional philanthropist, this large man with the large heart, for he laboured among poverty and vice from an innate desire to do good, and not from any hope that his works would be blazoned forth in the papers. He had no wife, no family, no relations, so he devoted his money, his time, and his talents to the service of paupers who could not afford to give anything in return except gratitude, and did not always give even that.

Of course, he had rich patients also. Oh, yes! many rich people came to Jacob Japix to be cured, and generally went away satisfied, for he was a clever physician, having the eye of a hawk and the intuition of a Galen for all kinds of mysterious diseases. But the money which the rich took from the poor in the way of scant payment for labour done went back to the pockets of the poor via Dr. Japix, so he illustrated in his own small way the law of compensation.

Mr. Fanks knew this doctor very well, having met him in connection with a celebrated poisoning case at Manchester, where he had attended as a witness in the character of an expert. Octavius, therefore, was very much delighted at chance having thrown Japix in his way for this special affair, as he was beginning to be troubled with vague fears the existence of which he persistently refused to acknowledge to himself.

Dr. Japix, being a big man, inhabited a big house just on the outskirts of the town, and on ringing a noisy bell, Octavius was admitted by a big footman, who said, in a big voice, that the Doctor was engaged at present, but would be at liberty soon. And soon it was, for just as the big footman was about to show Fanks into the waiting-room—on the right—a party of three (two ladies and one gentleman), accompanied by Japix, emerged from a door on the left.

One lady was tall, dark, and stately, with a serious cast of countenance; the other, small, fair, and vivacious, a veritable fairy, all sparkle and sunshine; and the gentleman was a long, lean man with a saturnine expression, not by any means prepossessing. Burly Dr. Japix with his big frame, his big voice, and his big laugh, accompanied the trio to the door, talking in a subdued roar the whole time.

"We'll set him up—set him up, Miss Florry, never fear—nerves—pooh! ha! ha! ha! nerves in a bridegroom. Who ever heard of such a thing?"

"Ah, but you see you're a bachelor," said the golden-haired fairy, gaily; "a horrid old bachelor, who doesn't know anything except how to give people nasty medicine."

"Hey! now, ha! ha! that's too bad. I always make your medicine nice. Wait till you're a matron, I'll make it nasty."

"When I'm a matron," said Miss Florry, demurely, "I'll take no medicine except Spolger's Soother," at which speech the Doctor laughed, the lean man scowled, and the two ladies attended by the scowl, departed, while the Doctor turned to greet his new visitor.

"Well, sir—well, sir—ha! may I be condemned to live on my own physic if it isn't M. Vidocq."

"Eh, my dear Doctor, me voici. Dumas, my dear physician; you've read 'The Three Musqueteers,' of course."

"Ha! ha! if you start quoting already," roared Japix, rolling ponderously into his study, followed by Fanks, "I give in at once; your memory, Mr. Thief-catcher, is cast-iron, and mine isn't. So I surrender at discretion. Now I'll be bound," continued the Doctor, waggishly, sitting in his huge chair, "you don't know where the quotation comes from."

"I don't," replied Fanks, after a moment's thought, sitting down; "you score one, my dear Doctor. By the way, don't call me Thief-catcher."

"Certainly not, Jonathan Wild."

"Nor that either."

"Why not, M. Fouche?"

"The third is the worst of all. At present I'm nothing but Mr. Rixton—my own name, Dr. Japix, as I told you."

"And Octavius Fanks?"

"Is in the Seventh Circle of Hell—at the back of the North Wind—in Nubibus—anywhere except where Mr. Rixton is."

"Ha! ha! hey! You're down here on business!"

"Private business."

"Ho! ho! and her name?"

"Mary Anne. She's a housemaid, and I love her, oh, I love her, and her heart I would discover! Pish! pshaw! 'Hence, vain deluding joys.' Milton, my dear Doctor! his best poem. But really, I want to be serious."

"Be serious, by all means," said Japix, complacently; "business first, pleasure afterwards. Dine with me to-night!"

"No, I've got an engagement. Say seven to-morrow, and I accept."

"'When found make a note of,'" remarked the Doctor, and scribbled a few lines in his memoranda-book. "Eh! Author?"

"Dickens' Captain Cuttle."

"Very good—go up top."

"Are you going to be serious?" said Fanks, in despair.

"My dear Rixton, I am serious," replied Dr. Japix, composing his features; "proceed!"

"First, who were the people who left as I came in?"

"Now what the deuce do you want to know that for?" said Japix, looking puzzled.

"Because I think one lady is Miss Judith Varlins, and the other Miss Florry Marson."

"Correct so far; but how the—"

"And the gentleman's name, Japix? The lean, lank man that looks like the Ancient Mariner in his shore clothes."

"Jackson Spolger, a patent medicine millionaire. Inherited it from Papa Spolger. Large fortune, disagreeable man, engaged to marry Miss Marson."

"Biography in a nutshell," said Fanks, calmly; "but surely not engaged."

"Why not? Are you in love with her yourself?"

"No; but I thought Sebastian Melstane—"

Dr. Japix uttered an ejaculation not complimentary to Mr. Melstane, and turned fiercely on Fanks.

"Sebastian Melstane be—"

"Don't," interrupted Octavius, holding up a warning hand; "perhaps he is already."

"What do you mean?"

"He is dead."

"Dead!"

"Yes; haven't you read the Jarlchester Mystery?"

"That suicide business. Of course; but I did not think—"

"The dead man was Melstane. Neither did I until an hour ago."

"How did you find out?" asked Japix, gravely.

"By means of this," answered Fanks, placing the pill-box on the table.

"Tonic pills," read Dr. Japix, wonderingly, "eh! Oh, yes, of course; I prescribed tonic pills for Melstane's nerves. But I don't see how you found out his name by this, nor how you connect the name of that scamp Melstane with the man who died at Jarlchester."

"Was Melstane a scamp?"

"Out and out," said Japix, emphatically.

"He must have been bad if you speak ill of him," observed Fanks, reflectively; "kind of man to have enemies, I suppose?"

"I should say plenty."

"Humph! I dare say."

"Dare say what? Talk about the Jarlchester Mystery, what are you?"

"A mystery also, eh, Doctor?" said Fanks, with a smile. "Well, I won't give you the trouble of guessing me. I'll explain myself."

The Doctor settled himself in his large chair, placed his large hands on each of his large knees, and observed in his large voice:

"Now then!"

Whereupon Octavius told him his experience during the Jarlchester inquest, suppressed the conversation and the name of Roger Axton, and finished up by describing how he had discovered the dead man's name from Wosk & Co.

"So you see, Japix," said the detective, decisively, "I saw your name on the prescription, and came at once to see you, as I want you to analyse these eight pills. According to your prescription, according to Mr. Wosk, according to the assistant, twelve pills were made up and delivered to Melstane. I can account for half of the twelve, so that ought to leave six; but in that box you will find eight. Now that is not right!"

"Certainly not!" remarked the Doctor, gravely regarding the pills; "six from twelve do not leave eight—at least, not by the rules of any arithmetic I'm acquainted with."

"So there are two extra pills."

"So I see! Two extra pills not made up by Wosk & Co."

"Now the question is," said Fanks, seriously, laying his hand on one of the Doctor's large knees, "the question is: What do those two extra pills mean?"

The Doctor said nothing, but looked inquiringly at the pill-box, as if he expected it to answer.

"I own," resumed Fanks, leaning back in his chair, "I own that I was half inclined to agree with the verdict of the jurors; it looked like suicide, but I had a kind of uneasy feeling that looks in this case were deceptive, so I thought I would like to know the name of the dead man, in order to find out if there was anything in his past life likely to lead him to self-destruction. I found the name, as I have told you, and I also discovered that there are two extra pills in that box, which have been added after it left the hands of Wosk & Co.—you understand."

"Perfectly."

"Now, those pills cannot have been added by Melstane, as he had no reason to do so. Twelve pills are enough for a man even with nerves, so why should he make those twelve into fourteen?"

"Ah, why, indeed?" said Japix, ponderously. "And your theory?"

"Is simply this. You say Melstane was a scamp; naturally he must have had enemies. Now I firmly believe that the two extra pills contain poison—say morphia, of which Melstane died—and they were placed in the box surreptitiously by one of his enemies."

"Natural enough."

"Melstane," continued Fanks, impressively, leaning forward, "took one of those extra pills, according to his usual custom, before going to bed, quite innocent of doing himself any harm. In the morning Melstane is found dead, and there is no evidence to show how he came by his death."

72

"Horrible! Horrible!"

"But observe," said Fanks, emphasizing his remarks with his forefinger, "observe how 'vaulting ambition o'er-leaps itself.' Again our divine William, Doctor. In other words, observe how the anxiety of the murderer to ensure the death of his victim has led to a danger of his own discovery. If he—I allude to the murderer—had put in one pill, making thirteen —which would have been a lucky number for our undiscovered criminal—the victim would have taken it, and absolutely no trace could have been discovered. Unluckily, however, for the criminal, he, afraid one morphia pill may not effectively do the work, puts in two morphia pills. Result, Sebastian Melstane, in perfect innocence, takes one and dies. The other pill—damning evidence, my dear Doctor —is one of the eight in that box, and I want you to analyse the whole eight pills in order to find that special one."

"And suppose I don't find it?" said Japix, putting the box on the table.

"In that case my theory falls to the ground, and Sebastian Melstane's death will remain a mystery to all men. But as sure as I sit here, Dr. Japix, you will find a deadly morphia pill among those seven harmless tonic pills."

"Your theory," remarked Japix, heavily, "is remarkably ingenious, and may—mind you, I don't say it is—but may be correct. I will analyse these pills, and let you know the result to-morrow. If I find here," said the Doctor, laying one massive hand on the pill-box, "if I find here a morphia pill, it will establish your theory in a certain sense."

"I think it will establish my theory in every sense," retorted Fanks, impetuously.

Dr. Japix shook his large head slowly, and delivered himself oracularly:

"Let us not," he said, looking at Fanks from under his shaggy eyebrows, "let us not jump to conclusions. I may find a morphia pill, but harmless."

"Deadly."

"Possibly harmless," said Japix, firmly.

"Probably deadly," rejoined Octavius, stubbornly.

"If deadly," continued the Doctor, quietly, "I grant your theory is a correct one, and that Sebastian Melstane met his death at the hands of the person who put those two extra pills in the box. If harmless, however," said Japix, raising his voice, "it establishes nothing. Melstane may have suffered from sleeplessness. Seeing his nerves were all wrong, I should say it was very probable he did, and taken morphia pills—purchased from, perhaps, a London chemist—in order to get a good night's rest."

"But why two morphia pills?" objected Octavius, earnestly. "Chemists don't sell morphia pills in twos."

"Your objection, sir, is not without some merit," said Japix, approvingly. "Still these two pills may have been the balance of another box, and placed in this one so as to obviate the trouble of carrying two boxes."

"Possible, certainly, but not probable. No, no, my dear Doctor, you need not try to upset my theory. Wait till you analyse those pills."

"I shall do so to-night, and to-morrow you will have my answer."

"I suppose you didn't give Melstane any morphia pills?" said Fanks, as he arose to take his leave.

"No; I don't believe in morphia pills for sleepless people, except in extreme cases. I generally give chloral, as I did to Mr. Jackson Spolger to-day."

"Oh, the Ancient Mariner," said Octavius, carelessly. "Does he suffer from sleeplessness?"

"Yes; on account of his approaching marriage, I presume."

"With Miss Marson?"

"Exactly."

"By the way," observed Fanks, suddenly, "was she not engaged to Melstane?"

"No, not engaged exactly," replied Japix, thoughtfully; "but she was in love with him. Strange how women adore scamps. But it's a long story, my dear Rixton. To-morrow night, when we both dine, across the walnuts and the wine, I'll tell to thee the tale divine. Ha, ha! you see I'm a poet, eh?"

"Yes, and a plagiarist also. The second line is Tennyson."

"Really, Mr. Bucket—Dickens, you observe—you're as sharp after a rhyme, as after a thief. With your active brain, I wonder you don't suffer from insomnia."

"When I do I'll come to you for morphia pills," said Octavius, laughing: "not the sort in that box, though. I don't want to die yet."

"I don't believe in morphia pills," remarked Japix, rising to accompany his guest to the door. "I never prescribe them.

Oh, yes, by the way, I did prescribe some for a Mr. Axton."

Octavius, who was going out of the door, turned suddenly round with a cry of horror.

"Roger Axton!"

"Yes; do you know him? Why, good gracious, what's the matter?"

For Octavius Fanks, trembling in every limb, had sunk into a chair near the door.

"Are you ill? Are you ill?" roared the Doctor, anxiously. "Here, let me get you some brandy."

"No, no!" said Fanks, recovering himself with a great effort, though his face was as pale as death. "I'm all right. I—I used to know Roger Axton, and the name startled me."

"Unpleasant associations," growled Japix, rubbing his large head in a vexed manner. "I hope not—dear, dear—I trust not. I liked the young fellow. A good lad—a very good lad."

Fanks at once hastened to dispel the Doctor's distrust.

"No! nothing unpleasant," he said, hurriedly: "he was my schoolfellow, and I haven't seen him for ten years."

Not a word about the meeting at Jarlchester, even to genial Dr. Japix, for the vague fears which had haunted the detective's mind were now taking a terrible shape—terrible to himself, more terrible to Roger Axton.

"I did not know Axton had been at Ironfields," he said at length, in a hesitating manner.

"Oh, yes, bless you! he was here for some time," cried Japix, cheerily; "I saw a good deal of him."

"What was his reason for staying down here?"

"Aha, aha!" thundered Japix, roguishly, "eh! you saw the reason leave my house to-day. A dark, queenly reason, and as good as gold."

"You allude to Miss Varlins."

"Of course. Ho! ho! 'Love's young dream.' Tommy Moore's remark, eh! 'Nothing half so sweet in life.' No doubt. I have no practical experience of it myself, being a bachelor; but Axton! ah! he thought Moore was right, I'll swear, when he was beside Judith Varlins."

Every word that dropped from the good Doctor's lips seemed to add to that hideous terror in the detective's mind, and he could hardly frame his next question, so paralysed he was by the fearful possibility of "what might be."

"I suppose she loves him?"

"Dear, dear! Now that's exactly what I don't know," said Japix, in a vexed tone; "she does and she doesn't. I was afraid she loved Mr. Scamp Melstane, you know. Women are riddles, eh—yes, worse than the Sphinx. She was with him a good deal, she wrote him letters and all that sort of thing, but it might have been friendship. I don't understand women, you see, I'm a bachelor."

This last speech of the Doctor's seemed too much for Octavius, and he felt anxious to get outside even into the fog and rain in order to breathe. He was so confused by what he had heard that he was afraid to open his lips, lest some word detrimental to his old schoolfellow should escape them. Hastily shaking the Doctor by the hand, he made a hurried promise to see him on the morrow.

"Fog and rain," roared the physician, as Octavius stepped outside; "must expect that now. Eh! ha! ho! ha! November smiles and November tears—principally tears. Yes. Don't forget to-morrow night—the pills—certainly. I will remember. Good-bye. Keep your feet dry. Warm feet and good repose, slam the door on the doctor's nose."

And Japix illustrated his little rhyme by slamming his own door, behind which his big voice could still be heard like distant thunder.

In the fog, in the rain, in the darkness, Octavius Fanks, stopping by a lighted shop-window, pulled out his pocket-book and looked at the memorandum—in shorthand—he had made of his conversation with Roger Axton.

In another moment he had restored the book to its former place, and from his lips there came a low cry of anguish:

"Oh, my old schoolfellow, has it come to this?"

Extracts From A Detectives Note-Book

"It is too terrible . . . I can't believe it . . . He did lie to me, as I thought . . . He has been to Ironfields. He knew the name of Melstane . . . What was he doing at Jarlchester? . . . Why was he there at the same time, in the same house as Melstane? . . . He must have known that the man who died was Melstane . . . He slept in the next room on the night of the murder . . . The door of Melstane's room was ajar in the morning . . . Could Roger have gone into the room and . . .

No, no; I can't believe it . . . He would not commit a crime . . . And yet he had morphia pills in his possession . . . What prevented him from getting two pills made extra strong . . . going into Melstane's room at night, and placing them in the box? . . . His motive for doing such a thing? . . . Dr. Japix supplies even that . . . He saw in Melstane a possible rival and wanted him out of the way . . . But what am I writing? . . . He cannot be guilty of this terrible crime . . . Yet everything points to it . . . his presence at Jarlchester . . . his possession of morphia . . . his evasive answers . . . I must find out the truth . . . I can't believe he would act thus, and yet . . .

"*Mem.*—To write to Axton's London address at once."

Chapter 6

Monsieur Judas is Confidential

A short distance from the mansion of Dr. Japix, on the road which ran from Ironfields to the dwellings of the magnates of the city, stood a large, square stone house in a dreary piece of ground. The house itself was also remarkably dreary, being painted a dull gray, with all the windows and doors dismally picked out in black. Two stories it was, with five windows in the top story facing the road, four windows and a door with a porch in the lower, and still deeper down the basements guarded at the sides of the house by spiky iron railings of a most resentful appearance.

The garden in front had a broad walk running down to a rusty iron gate, on either side a plot of rank green grass, and in the centre of each churchyard-looking plot a tall, solemn cypress. The four lower windows opened like doors directly on to the grass-plots, but were always closed, as Mrs. Binter (proprietress of this charming establishment) thought egress by the funereal front door was quite sufficient.

Over the porch was a broad whiteboard, whereon was inscribed in grim black letters, "Binter's Boarding-house," and although the sight of the unwholesome house was enough to scare timid mortals, Binter's was generally well stocked, and the proprietress did fairly well in her particular line of overcharging and underfeeding.

A tall, gaunt, grim person was Mrs. Binter, arrayed in a severe-looking dress of a dull gray colour (like the house), and picked out in black (also like the house) by wearing an inky ribbon round her throat, a jet-trimmed gauze cap on her iron-gray hair, and rusty black mittens on her lean hands. She also wore round her narrow waist a thin belt of black leather, attached to which by a steel chain was a large bunch of keys, which so jingled when she walked, that in the twilight one could easily believe that Binter's was haunted by a gaunt ghost clanking its rusty chain through the dreary passages.

Mrs. Binter's papa (long since deceased) had been a warder in the county jail, and his one fair daughter having been brought up with an intimate knowledge of prison life, had so accustomed herself to view the world through the bars of a jail, that she had become quite imbued with the routine, the traditions, and the spirit of a first-class penitentiary. It might have been hereditary, it might have been habitual, but Mrs. Binter was certainly very jail-like in all her ways.

80

Having captured Mr. Binter (who had no mind of his own), she made him marry her, and for the rest of his life relegated him to the basement, where he did all the work of a "boots" without the wages of one. His wife looked after the boarders, whom she treated like prisoners, presiding at her own table, where the food was very plain and very wholesome, seeing that they were in bed in their little cells at a proper hour, and altogether conducting the establishment in as near a manner approaching the paternal system as she was able.

Binter's was usually full, as Mrs. B. always advertised it as being in the country, and the worked-to-death clerks of Ironfields were glad to get a breath of fresh air, even when attended by the inconvenience of living in a private jail. But in the evenings all the prison-boarders generally went out on a kind of ticket-of-leave (the understanding being that they were to be in before midnight), and Mrs. Binter had the whole of her private jail to herself.

On this evening, however, all the boarders had gone out with the exception of Monsieur Judas, who was seated in a little cell (called by courtesy the drawing-room), before a feeble little fire which cowered in a large, cold grate. The room was scantily furnished in a very substantial fashion, the chairs very straight in the backs, the sofa just short enough to prevent any one lying down comfortably, the floor covered with a black and white diamond oilcloth, cold and slippery, with a narrow strip of woollen matting in front of the fire. If Mrs. Binter could have chained the fireirons to the wall (after the most approved prison fashion), she no doubt would have been glad to do so; but as she had to preserve a certain appearance of freedom (for which she was profoundly sorry), she let them lie loose, and Monsieur Judas was now sitting with the tongs in his hand adding little bits of coal to the shivering fire.

Mrs. Binter having ascertained through one of the head-warders (the housemaid) that Monsieur Judas was going to stay in all the evening, regarded this as an infringement of the ticket-of-leave system, and went up to the drawing-room cell to speak to him.

Judas heard the rattle of the keys, and knew the head-jailer was coming along, but without desisting from his employment he raised his crafty eyes to the gaunt figure that speedily stood before him.

"Ain't you goin' out?" queried the gaunt figure, folding its arms, that is, the fingers of each hand grasped the elbows of the other arm.

"De fogs is too moch," responded Judas, picking up another bit of coal, "an' I am chez moi for a frien'."

"Oh, that's it, munseer," said the head-jailer, rattling her keys, "you're expectin' of a friend! Why ain't you goin' back to the shop?"

"Eh! ma chère, non! I am home to-ni."

"You'll want the fire, I suppose," remarked Mrs. Binter, grudgingly, as if she would like to take it away with her, "an' the lamp. I was goin' to put 'em both out, but if you must, you must. Would your friend like supper?"

"Je ne sais pas," said Monsieur Judas, putting down the tongs and shrugging his shoulders. "No! I do no so tink."

"Supper's extra, you know," observed Mrs. Binter, determined to have out of the supper what she was losing in the lamp and fire; "but it ain't hospital to let a friend go away without a bite. It may be French manners," added the jailer with scathing irony, "but it ain't English."

Monsieur Judas spread out his hands with a deprecating gesture, murmured something indistinct, and then relapsed into silence, much to the disappointment of Mrs. Binter.

"There's two legs of a fowl," said the lady, rattling her keys. "Binter was goin' to have 'em for his breakfast; but I can trim 'em up with parsley, if you like, an' with bread an' cheese an' a bottle of that sour vinegar you call Julia, it'll be quite a little 'oliday for you."

Just at this moment the bell rang, and Mrs. Binter hastening to the front door, admitted Mr. Fanks, took him in charge, and having delivered him over to the safe custody of Monsieur Judas, retired with a final rattle of the keys in deep wrath at her failure with the supper idea.

Octavius, who looked rather pale, but with a stern expression on his face, slipped off his fur coat, and having surveyed Judas with a calculating expression, sat down by the fiction of a fire, the Frenchman taking a seat opposite.

"I do wait for you," said Monsieur Judas, smoothing one lean hand with the other, and letting his eyelids droop over his crafty eyes.

"Speak French," replied Fanks, in that language; "we'll understand one another better if you do."

"Eh, certainly, my friend," said Judas, rapidly, "it is easier for me. You speak French very well; eh, yes, very well, monsieur."

Fanks acknowledged this compliment with a stiff nod, and plunged at once into the object of his visit.

"Now, Monsieur Guinaud, about your friend, Melstane?"

"Eh! a moment, if you please," hissed Judas, in his low, soft voice, holding up his hand. "Before we speak of the poor Melstane let us understand each other, monsieur. That is but right, my friend."

"Yes, it is but right; what do you want to know?"

Monsieur Judas placed his elbows on his knees, warmed his claw-like hands over the fire, and looked cunningly at the detective before speaking.

"Your name, monsieur?"

"Rixton."

"It is very well—that name, Monsieur Fanks," replied Judas, with a mocking smile.

"You know my real name, I see," rejoined Octavius, without moving a muscle of his face. "I compliment you on your penetration."

"Eh, it is not much," said the Frenchman, with a deprecatory shrug. "Monsieur Vosk he read to me the papers of Jarlcesterre, and I find one Monsieur Fanks, agent of the police, to be present. He has the box which my poor friend had for the pills. A stranger comes to me and shows the same box, and I say: 'Monsieur Fanks.' Is that not so?"

"Well, you've read the papers," observed Fanks, slowly, "and know all the circumstances of your friend's death."

"The papers say he gave himself the death, monsieur."

"And what do you say?"

84

"Eh, I do not know," replied Monsieur Judas, shrugging his shoulders, and opening his eyes to their fullest extent (the guileless look). "What is the opinion of monsieur?"

Mr. Fanks thought a moment or two before replying. He wanted to find out all about Melstane's past life, and no one could tell him so much as the fellow-lodger of the dead man. Judas, however, was no ordinary man, and would not speak freely unless he knew the whole circumstances of the case. Now Fanks did not trust Judas in any way. He did not like his appearance, nor his manner, nor anything about him, and would have preferred him to remain in ignorance of his (Fanks') suspicions. But as he could not find out what he wanted to know without telling Judas his suspicions, and as he could not tell Judas his suspicions without letting him know more than he cared to, Octavius was rather in a dilemma.

Guinaud saw this and put an end to this hesitation in a most emphatic fashion.

"Monsieur, I see, does not trust me," he said, with an injured air. "Monsieur would know all and tell nothing. But no, certainly that will not be pleasing to me. Figure to yourself, monsieur. I am a Frenchman, me, I am a man of honour, is it not so? Monsieur knows all of the case; but I—eh! I may know something of good also. If monsieur shows me his heart, the heart of Jules Guinaud is open to him. There it is."

Not the heart of Monsieur Guinaud, but the statement of Monsieur Guinaud's feelings; so Fanks, seeing that he must either give confidence for confidence or remain ignorant, chose the former alternative, and spoke out.

"Very well, I will tell you what I think, but of course you will keep our conversation secret."

Judas blew an airy kiss with a light touch of the long fingers on his mouth, and laughed pleasantly.

"My faith, yes. Monsieur is the soul of honour, and I, Monsieur Fanks—eh, is it not the name?—I am the resemblance of that soul. What you speak this night drops into the open heart of me. Snip, as say you English, I close the heart. The talk is safe; but, yes—you understand."

"Then that's all right," said Fanks, grimly; "we may as well proceed to business. As Mr. Vosk translated to you, the papers say Melstane committed suicide—gave himself the death! Comprehend you, eh? Very well. I say no. It was a crime! Melstane was murdered."

"And by whom, monsieur?"

"That's what I've got to find out."

"And the opinion of monsieur?"

"I will explain. Melstane had a box of tonic pills with him, containing, when it left your shop, twelve pills."

"It is true, monsieur, twelve pills."

"I can account for six pills, and in the box at present there are eight."

"I understand," said Judas, quickly. "Two pills were placed in the box by an unknown. Those two pills contained poison. The poor Melstane took one pill of poison, and died. Monsieur has taken the pills to Monsieur the Dr. Japix to find the other pill."

"You are perfectly right," said Fanks, rather astonished at the rapidity with which the assistant grasped the case.

"Eh, monsieur, I am not blind," replied Judas, shrugging his shoulders; "and now monsieur desires to find the unknown who placed the pills of poison in the box."

"Exactly! And to do so I want you to tell me all you know about Sebastian Melstane's life here," answered Fanks, producing his secretive little note-book.

Monsieur Guinaud looked thoughtfully at the fire, then glanced up at the ceiling, and at length brought his eyes (guileless expression) to rest on the face of Mr. Fanks.

"It is difficult to make the commencement," he said, speaking slowly, as if he weighed every word. "Behold, monsieur, I make the story to myself this way: My poor Sebastian, he is an artist. Eh! not what you call a great artist for the Salon in London, but good in the pictures. Oh! yes, much of the talent. Six months ago, in London, he beholds a pretty lady. It is Mees Mar-rson, the daughter of the very rich monsieur of this town. My friend has the grand passion for the charming mees—eh! I believe it well—and comes to this town to say 'I love you!' Alas, he finds that the too charming mees is to marry the rich Monsieur Sp—Sp—I cannot say your English names."

"Spolger!"

"But certainly that is the name. Yes! she is to marry this rich monsieur; but my brave Sebastian, he mocks himself of that. Here in this house he stays, and I make myself his friendship. He tells me all his love. The father of my charming mees is enraged, and forbids my friend to look, to see, to speak with the beautiful child. But she has a heart, this angel, and loves to distraction the handsome boy, my friend. They meet, they talk, they write the letters, and monsieur the father knows nothing. Then to this pension there comes Monsieur Axton."

"Roger Axton?" said Fanks, biting his lips.

"Yes, truly! You know him? Eh! it is strange," said Judas, inquisitively.

"It is well, it is well, I know him," replied Fanks, waving his hand impatiently; "go on, Monsieur Guinaud."

"Very well! This Monsieur Roger has the love for the beautiful Mees Var-rlins! Eh! you understand? He goes to the house, and is a friend of monsieur the father. The poor Sebastian and this monsieur have not the friendship. Monsieur Roger tells the dear Mees Var-rlins of the meetings of Mees Mar-rson and my friend. Mees Mar-rson is taken away to the Ile de Vite; Monsieur Roger also goes in August. The brave Sebastian, he mocks himself, and moves not. When they return, Mees Var-rlins is the chaperon of the angel, and she meets not my friend. This Sebastian insults Monsieur Roger as a spy—a villain, and Monsieur Roger departs in October."

"Departs for what place?" asked Fanks, making a note of the month in his book.

"I do not know," replied Judas, with a characteristic shrug; "Monsieur Roger is not my friend. In November, my Sebastian, he says to me: 'It is well; I go to Jarlcesterre.'"

"What did he mean by 'it is well'?"

"But, monsieur, I am in darkness. Yes, truly. He had visited the house of Monsieur le Pilule."

"You mean Spolger's house?"

"Yes! He sees Monsieur le Pilule to speak of his love for Mees Mar-rson. When he returns to this pension, he says: 'It is well; I go to Jarlcesterre'—no more. Then my friend, the brave Sebastian, goes to Jarlcesterre, and I see him not more."

"An interview between Melstane and Spolger could hardly have been satisfactory," said Fanks, looking keenly at the Frenchman.

"Eh, monsieur, I know nothing of that," answered Judas, with his guileless look.

"Why did Melstane go to Jarlchester, of all places in the world?"

"I have told monsieur everything," said Monsieur Cuinaud, with oily politeness.

"Humph! I'm doubtful of that," muttered Fanks, thoughtfully. "And is that all you know?"

"Eh! what would you?"

"It doesn't throw any light on the murder."

"Wait, monsieur," said Judas, earnestly, "a moment. One night before my friend went away, Mees Var-rlins stop her carriage at the shop. She comes in to me and says: 'I cannot get a stamp of postage. Have you a stamp of postage?' I say 'yes,' and give her a stamp of postage. She places the stamp of postage on a letter, and goes away in the carriage. I see the letter."

"And the name on the letter?"

"Monsieur Roger Axton, Jarlcesterre," said Judas, quietly; "now! eh! you see?"

"I see nothing," replied Fanks, bluntly. "Miss Varlins wrote to Axton at Jarlchester. What of that? I know Axton was at Jarlchester; I saw him there."

"Is that so?" said Monsieur Judas, eagerly; "then, behold,

monsieur! Axton is at Jarlcesterre; Melstane goes down also to Jarlcesterre. Before he goes," pursued Judas, bending forward and speaking in a whisper, "he buy pills of morphia! eh! is that not so? My friend and Axton are enemies. At Jarlcesterre they meet; the poor Melstane dies of morphia! What would you?"

"Do you mean to say that Roger Axton murdered Melstane?" cried Fanks, trying to control himself.

Monsieur Judas spread out his hands once more.

"I say nothing, monsieur. But because of Miss Mar-rson they fight—they fight desperate. Axton has the pills of morphia. Melstane dies of the pills of morphia! But no, I say nothing."

"I think you've said quite enough," retorted Fanks, coldly. "I don't believe what you say."

"Monsieur!"

"Don't ruffle your feathers, Monsieur Guinaud; I mean what I say, and in order to prove it, I'll ask Roger Axton to come down here and give his version of the story."

"He can but say what I declare."

"That's a matter of opinion."

"Monsieur?"

"Sir."

The two men had risen to their feet, and were standing opposite to one another; Fanks cold and scornful, Judas visibly agitated, with his eyes narrowed down into a dangerous expression. He looked like a snake preparing for a spring, and Fanks was on his guard; but at length, with a hissing laugh, Judas stepped back and bowed submissively.

"Let us not fight, I pray you, monsieur," he said, gently; "when Monsieur Axton comes you will see that I speak truly."

"Till that time comes," replied Octavius, putting on his coat, "we need not meet."

"As monsieur please."

"Good-bye, Monsieur Guinaud."

"Au revoir, monsieur."

"I said good-bye."

"Eh! yes! I replied 'Au revoir,' monsieur."

Octavius turned on his heel without another word, and left the room. In the passage he met Mrs. Binter, hovering round in the hope of supper being ordered. She at once took Fanks in charge, and conducting him to the door, released him from prison with manifest reluctance.

Meanwhile Monsieur Judas, left alone, was leaning against the mantelpiece with a smile on his evil face.

"Eh! Monsieur Axton," he said to himself, in a whisper, "you gave me the insult. To-night I have paid the debt—in part! Wait, Monsieur Axton; wait, Meess Var-rlins; I hold you both. It is I, Jules Guinaud, that can strike—when I wish."

Extracts From A Detective's Note-Book

"I don't believe second thoughts are best. I always go by first impressions . . . My first impressions of Judas—I give him his nickname—are bad . . . He's a slimy scoundrel, very difficult to deal with . . . In our interview of to-night I had to tell him more than I cared he should know . . . But it was my only chance of finding out anything . . . What I did find out looks very bad for Roger Axton . . . He was at Ironfields, in spite of his denial . . . He stayed at Binter's boarding-house, and knew Melstane intimately . . . I learn from Judas that they quarrelled bitterly . . . This is very bad . . . Roger left Ironfields in a rage against Melstane . . . When next seen he is down at Jarlchester in the same house as Melstane . . . He has a grudge against Melstane, and while he is under the same roof Melstane dies . . . God forgive me if I should be suspecting my old schoolfellow wrongfully, but things look very suspicious against him . . . Another thing I learned from Judas, viz., that Miss Varlins corresponded with Roger at Jarlchester.

"Query! Can she know anything about the death?

"I have written to Axton, asking him to come down here and see me . . . If he refuses, I'm afraid my suspicions will be confirmed . . . I wish I could disbelieve Judas . . . He looks a secretive scoundrel . . . and yet his story against Roger is confirmed by my own experience . . . I think—no, I dare not think . . . I will wait to hear the other side of the story from Axton . . ."

Chapter 7

An Unwilling Bride

Francis Marson was one of the most prominent men in Ironfields, owing to his immense wealth, his clear head, and his personal attributes. His father, a keen man of business, had been born and bred in the little village from which Ironfields had sprung, and when the discovery of iron in the vicinity had laid the foundations of the present world-renowned town, Francis Marson the elder had been one of the first to profit by the discovery. He watched his opportunity, bought land (with borrowed money) on which he believed rich veins of iron ore might be found, and when they were found, built a foundry, turned over the money, paid back what he had borrowed, and was soon on the high road to fortune. When firmly established he sent his only son to college, and then took him into the business, which henceforward was known as that of Marson & Son. In the fulness of time he was gathered to his fathers, and Francis Marson the younger stepped into the enjoyment of unlimited wealth.

The younger Marson (now iron-gray, severe, and stately) married the only daughter of Sir Miles Canton, of Canton Hall, and on the death of the old baronet that property came into the possession of Mr. and Mrs. Marson, who henceforth took up their residence in the old Tudor mansion.

Fortune having been thus kind to Francis Marson, thought it well to remind him that complete happiness was not the lot of any mortal, so robbed him of his wife, who died some years after giving birth to Florence Marson. On her death-bed, the young mother confided the child to her husband, and implored him to bring her up with Judith Varlins, the daughter of a distant relation. Judith, who was at that time twelve years of age and grave beyond her years, took this so to herself that little Florry was confided to her care, and henceforth devoted her life to the guardianship of the six-year-old child. Francis Marson, broken down by grief, went away on his travels, and the two children grew up together, went to school together, and when their school-days were over returned to Canton Hall in company with its master.

Now Florry Marson was a charming, golden-haired fairy of twenty years of age, while Judith was a stately brunette some six years older. Blonde and brunette, day and night, dark and fair, they were both equally charming in their own way, but as different in disposition as in appearance. Judith was mistress of the Hall, looked after the servants, received the company, and in fact acted as the elder sister, while Florry, bright-eyed and frivolous, did nothing but amuse herself. Francis Marson was fond of both the girls, but simply worshipped Florry, who lighted up the whole house like a sunbeam. Both Judith and the father combined to spoil her, and up to the age of twenty the life of Florry had been nothing but pleasure, gaiety, and sunshine.

Then came the episode of Sebastian Melstane, who had met Florry in London, and she, reckless in all things, had given away her frivolous little heart to this handsome, dark-haired artist. On making inquiries, Mr. Marson had found out sufficient about Mr. Melstane's past life to make him resolve his darling should never marry such a scamp, and he forbade Florry to think of him. Upon which Miss Florry, with her silly little head stuffed full of poetry and romance, regarded Melstane as a persecuted hero, and on his coming to Ironfields met him by stealth, wrote him letters, exchanged presents, and in fact did everything a foolish girl would do when flattered and loved by a romantic scamp.

Roger Axton, knowing Melstane's bad character, had put an end to these stolen meetings by telling Judith, and Florry was carried off to Ventnor. While there she still sighed after her lover, and when she returned to Ironfields saw him with difficulty, as Judith was too vigilant to let her remain long out of her sight. Then Melstane went to Jarlchester, and Florry said to Judith with many tears and sighs that she would be true to him, although she had now been engaged for some time to Mr. Jackson Spolger, the son of a man who had made his money out of a patent medicine.

Francis Marson had set his heart on this match, and although Florry violently protested against it, insisted that she should become engaged to Mr. Spolger, as he was anxious to place her beyond the power of Sebastian Melstane, and, moreover, Jackson Spolger was too wealthy a suitor to be rejected lightly.

Some days after Fanks' visit to Monsieur Judas at the end of November, Judith and Florry were both in the drawing-room of the Hall having afternoon tea.

It was a large, handsome apartment, furnished with great artistic taste, principally due to Miss Varlins, who had a wonderful eye for colour and effect. A curiously carved oaken ceiling, walls draped with dark red velvet which fell in heavy folds to the velvet pile carpet of the same colour, plenty of sombre pictures in oil in tarnished gilt frames, many small tables covered with nicknacks (selected by frivolous Florry), numbers of comfortable lounging-chairs, inviting repose, and a handsome grand piano littered with loose music (Florry again)—it was truly a delightful room. Then there were cabinets of rare china, monstrous jars of quaint design and bizarre colours, and flowers, flowers, flowers everywhere. Both ladies had a perfect passion for flowers, and even in this bleak month of November the most exquisite exotics were to be seen throughout the room in profusion, filling the air with their heavy odours.

Four windows at the other end of the room looked out on to the garden, but were now closed, for it was a cold afternoon, and the driving rain beat against the glass and on the leafless trees outside. A blazing fire in the old fashioned fireplace with its quaint Dutch tiles, a low table drawn near the hearth, on which stood the tea service, and Miss Varlins in a chair knitting quietly, while Florry flitted about the room like a restless fairy in the waning light.

A handsome woman, Judith Varlins, with a proud, dark face, and a somewhat stern expression, which always relaxed to tenderness when it rested on the diminutive form of Florry. And that young lady was very tiny, more like a piece of Dresden china than anything else, with her delicate complexion, her piquant face, glittering golden hair, and dainty figure. Clothed in white—Miss Marson always affected white—in some lacy material, soft and delicate like a cobweb, she formed a strong contrast to the sombre beauty of Judith in her plain, black silk dress.

And the little figure went flitting here and there, now at the windows, looking out into the chill twilight, then bending over some great bunch of flowers inhaling the perfume, at the piano striking a few random chords, hovering round the tea table, flashing into the red firelight, melting into the cold shadows, like to some will-o'-the-wisp, some phantom, some restless shadow rather than anything of this earth.

"Florry, my pet," said Judith, at length, pausing in her knitting, "you will tire yourself running about so much."

Whereupon the fairy floated airily towards the fire, and settled lightly down, like thistledown, on a footstool, where she sat clasping her knees with her arms with a cross expression of countenance, a very discontented fairy indeed.

"For really," she said, at length, pursuing a train of thought that was in her shallow mind, "to be called Spolger—Mrs. Jackson Spolger. It's horrid! so is he. The monster!"

"Florry, Florry! don't talk like that about your future husband," remonstrated Judith; "it's not nice, my dearest."

"Neither is he," retorted Miss Marson, resting her chin on her knees and staring into the fire; "he's so lean, like a skeleton, and so crabbed—oh, so crabbed."

"But he loves you, dear."

"Yes, like a dog loves a bone. I know he's one of those men who hit their wives over the head with a poker; he looks like a poker man. I wish he was Sebastian, and Sebastian was he."

"Don't talk about Sebastian, my dear Florence," said Miss Varlins, severely—that is, as severely as she could to Florry; "your father would never have agreed to your marrying such a scamp!"

"He's no worse than other people," muttered Florry, rebelliously.

"I don't know about other people," replied Judith, coldly; "but I'm certain Sebastian Melstane would have made you a bad husband. However, he's gone now, and you'll never see him again."

"Never!"

"No, never! Mr. Melstane has passed out of your life entirely," said Judith, looking steadily at Florry, who appeared to be rather scared.

"What horrid things you say, Judith, you horrid thing," she whimpered, at length. "I don't know why Sebastian went away, and I don't know why he hasn't written to me. I thought he loved me, but if he had, he would have written. But he'll come back and explain everything."

"I'm certain he won't!" answered Judith, sternly.

"Why are you certain?"

"I have my reasons," said Judith, quietly.

It might have been the twilight or the dancing shadows of the fire, but as she spoke her face seemed to grow old and haggard for the moment, even to Miss Marson's unobservant eyes. Florry with her own blue eyes wide open, a terrified expression on her face, and a tremulous under-lip, suddenly burst into tears, and rising from her footstool, flung herself on her knees at the feet of her cousin, sobbing violently.

"Come, come!" said Miss Varlins, smoothing the golden head as it lay in her lap. "I did not mean to speak severely; but really, Florry, I was very sorry that Mr. Melstane loved you."

"I—I can't help it if he did," sobbed Florry, passionately; "it's not my fault if people will love me. There's Mr. Spolger—he's always making love, and that horrid, red-haired Frenchman; every time I go out he never takes his eyes off my face."

"What! that man at Wosk's?" cried Judith, with great indignation. "Surely he has not such impertinence!"

"No, he hasn't," replied Florry, sitting up and drying her eyes; "but he will look at me in such a way. I'm sure he's in love with me—the horrid thing."

"He was a friend of Mr. Melstane's, I believe," said Judith, angrily, "and you, no doubt, saw him during those foolish meetings with that man."

"No, I didn't," answered Florry, going back to her footstool; "I never saw him at all. And our meetings weren't foolish. I love Sebastian very much, only papa will make me marry this horrid Spolger thing."

"How many times did you see Mr. Melstane?"

"Five or six times here and once in London.

"Florry!"

"Well!" said Miss Marson, pettishly, "you asked me? I saw him in London that day I went to see Aunt Spencer, when we stopped in London on our way to Ventnor."

"Why didn't Aunt Spencer tell me of it, then?"

"She didn't know," answered Florry, penitently. "I met Sebastian on the way, and we were together for two hours. Then I went on to Aunt Spencer and told her nothing."

"And told me nothing also," said Judith, severely. "Upon my word, Florry, I did not think you were so deceitful! You met Mr. Melstane in London, and this is the first I hear about it."

"Well, you were so horrid, Judith," pouted Florry, playing with her handkerchief; "and Sebastian told me to say nothing."

"He's a bad man!"

"No, he's not," retorted Miss Marson, angrily; "he's a very nice man, and I love him very, very much, in spite of Mr. Spolger—there!"

Judith was about to make some angry reply, feeling thoroughly disgusted at Florry's duplicity, when the door was thrown open, and Mr. Marson entered the room.

A tall, severe-looking man, this Francis Marson, with a worn, worried expression on his face. He sighed wearily as he sat down near the fire.

"Oh, what a sigh—what a big sigh!" cried Florry, recovering her spirits and poising herself on the old man's knee. "What is the matter, papa?"

"Nothing, child, nothing," replied Marson, hastily, smoothing the golden hair of his darling. "Business worries, my dear; what I spoke about the other day."

"Oh!"

Florry drew down the corners of her mouth as if she were going to cry; then, suddenly changing her mind, she threw her arms round her father's neck, and placed her soft face against his withered cheek.

"Don't talk about business, papa," she said, coaxingly; "I hate it; it's so disagreeable."

"So it is for a frivolous young person like you, dear," said Mr. Marson, cheerfully; "but it's very necessary all the same. What would become of your thousand and one wants but for this same business you so disapprove of?"

"Oh, I wish I had a fairy purse," cried Florry, clapping her hands, "with a gold piece in it every time I opened it. It would save such a lot of trouble."

"A fairy world," said Mr. Marson, looking at her fondly; "that is what you would like. And you the lovely princess whom the handsome prince comes to awaken."

"Well, Florry has a prince," said Judith, quietly; "the Prince of the Gold Mines!"

She had not been paying much attention to the conversation between father and daughter, as she was evidently thinking deeply, and her thoughts, judging from the severe expression of her countenance, were not particularly pleasant. The last words of Mr. Marson, however, enchained her attention, and she made the remark about the prince on purpose to see if the old man knew how disagreeable the Spolger alliance was to his child.

"A prince!" echoed Florry, tossing her head. "And what a prince! He's more like an ogre."

"A very devoted ogre, at all events," said Judith, significantly.

"Spolger's a good fellow," observed Marson, hurriedly; "a little rough, perhaps, but his heart is in the right place. Beauty is only skin-deep."

"I suppose you mean—" began Florry, when her father interrupted her quickly.

"Florry," he said, angrily, "I forbid you to mention that man's name. I would sooner see you in your grave than married to Sebastian Melstane."

"There's no chance of that occurring now," interjected

Judith, with sombre earnestness.

The fairy looked from one to the other with a scared expression of countenance, and seeing how severe they both looked, subsided into a white heap on the hearthrug, and burst into tears.

"How horrid you are, papa," she cried, dismally; "and so is Judith. I'm sure Mr. Melstane's very nice. He's so handsome, and talks so beautifully about poetry. He's like Conrad, and Mr. Spolger isn't, and I wish I was dead with a tombstone and a broken heart," concluded Miss Marson, tearfully.

Judith looked at Mr. Marson, and he looked at Judith. They both felt quite helpless in dealing with this piece of frivolity, whose very weakness constituted her strength. At last Mr. Marson, bending down, smoothed Florry's hair fondly, and spoke soothingly to her.

"My dear child," he said, quietly, "you know that all I desire is your happiness; and, believe me, you will thank me in after life for what I am now doing. Sebastian Melstane is a scamp and a spendthrift. If you married him, he would neglect you and make you miserable. Jackson Spolger will make you a good husband, and protect a delicate flower like you from the bleak winds of adversity."

"But he's so ugly," sobbed Florry, childishly; "just like the what's-his-name in 'Notre Dame.'"

"If you have such an aversion to marry him, Florry, then don't do it," said Judith, quietly. "I'm sure your father would not force you into a marriage against your will."

"By no means," said Marson, hastily. "I placed the case before you the other day, Florry, and I place it now. As you know, I have had great losses lately, and unless I can obtain a large sum of ready money I will be irretrievably ruined. Jackson Spolger has promised to put money into the business if you become his wife. I told you this, and you consented, so it is childish of you to go on like this, If you dislike Spolger so much, I will not force you to marry him; but I warn you that your refusal means ruin."

"You won't let me marry Sebastian Melstane," cried Florry, obstinately.

"No, I won't," retorted her father, angrily. "You need not marry Mr. Spolger unless you like, but you—you certainly shall not marry Sebastian Melstane with my consent; I would rather see you in your grave."

"Then I suppose I must marry Mr. Spolger," said Florry, dolefully drying her eyes.

"That is as you please," replied Marson, rising to his feet and walking slowly to and fro. "I don't want to sell my child for money. I simply place the case before you, and you are free to refuse or accept as you please. Yes means prosperity, no means ruin, and the choice is entirely in your hands."

Florry said nothing, but sat on the hearthrug twisting her handkerchief and staring at the fire.

"I would like to say one word, Florry," said Judith, bending forward. "If you did not intend to marry Mr. Spolger you should have said so at first; now the wedding-day is fixed for next week, your dresses are ready, the guests are invited, so it would be rather hard on the poor man to dash the cup of happiness from his lips just as he is tasting it."

"Nevertheless," said Marson, stopping in his walk, "late as it is, Florry, if you think that you cannot make Jackson Spolger a good wife, I will break off the match without delay."

"But that means ruin," cried Florry, tearfully.

"Yes!" said Marson, curtly, "ruin."

Florry sat thinking as deeply as her shallow little brain would allow her. She saw plainly that if she refused to marry Mr. Spolger, she would never gain her fathers consent to her marriage with Melstane, and as a refusal meant ruin without any chance of obtaining the wish of her heart, she did not see what was to be gained by being perverse. Shallow, frivolous, selfish as she was, she saw all this quite plainly, and, moreover, being too timid to brook her father's displeasure, she made up her mind to yield. Rising to her feet, she stole towards her father, as he stood in gloomy silence looking out on the wintry lawn, and threw her arms round his neck.

"Papa," she whispered, "I will marry Mr. Spolger."

"Of your own free will?" he asked, a trifle sternly.

"Of my own free will," she repeated, steadily. "I am sorry for Sebastian, for I do love him; but I don't want to vex you, dearest, so I'll be awfully nice to Mr. Spolger and marry him next week."

"My dearest," said Marson, in a tone of great relief, "you don't know how happy you have made me."

"Florry," cried Judith, rolling up her work.

"Yes, Judith," said Florry, leaving her father, and coming to her cousin.

"You are quite sure you mean what you say?" asked Miss Varlins, looking at her steadily.

"Quite sure."

"No more tears or crying after Sebastian?"

"Don't talk of Sebastian," said Florry, angrily. "I'll marry Mr. Spolger, and I dare say he'll make me happy."

Judith said no more, but resumed her work with a sigh; but Mr. Marson, coming towards the fire, was about to speak, when the door opened and a footman announced: "Mr. Jackson Spolger."

Chapter 8

Mr. Spolger Tells a Story

Jackson Spolger, proprietor of that celebrated patent medicine, "Spolger's Soother," was a long, lean, lank man, with a somewhat cross face, and a mildly irritable manner. Spolger the father had been a chemist, but having invented the "Soother," made his fortune thereby, owing to lavish advertising and plenty of testimonials (paid for) from hypochondriacal celebrities. Having thus fulfilled his mission in this world, and benefited his fellow men by the "Soother," he departed therefrom, leaving his money and his "Soother" to Spolger the son, who still carried on the advertising business, and derived a large income from it. He had been well educated, had travelled a good deal, and had a kind of social veneer, which, added to his money, entitled him to be called a gentleman. Although he suffered a good deal from ill-health, he never by any chance used the "Soother," which led ill-natured people to remark that it was made to sell and not to cure. Mr. Spolger, however, did not mind ill-natured people being too much taken up with himself and his ailments, of which he was always talking. He chatted constantly about his own liver, or some one else's liver, prescribed remedies, talked gloomily of his near death, and altogether was not a particularly agreeable person.

Being thus a diseased egotist, he carried his mania for health even into his matrimonial prospects, and loved Florry not so much on account of her beauty as because she looked delicate, and in a wife of such a constitution he thought he would always have some one beside him, on whom to practise his little curative theories. He always carried in his pocket a horrible little book called "Till the Doctor Comes," and was never so delighted as when he found some one sufficiently ill who would permit him to prescribe one of the remedies from his precious book. He preferred a chemist's shop to his own house, loved doctors above all other men, and contemplated passing his honeymoon in a hydropathic establishment, where there would be plenty of fellow-sufferers with whom to compare notes.

At present he was clad in a heavy tweed suit, and wore a thickly lined fur coat, galoshes on his feet, and a roll of red flannel round his throat.

"How do you do, Mr. Marson?" he said, in a thin, irritable voice, as he shook hands. "I hope you are well. You don't look it. Your hand is moist; that's a bad sign. Dry? Yes, mine is dry. I'm afraid it's fever. Diseases are so subtle. Miss Varlins, you look healthy. Florry, my dearest, what a thin dress for this weather!"

107

"Oh, it's all right, Mr. Spolger."

"Jackson," he interpolated.

"It's all right, Jackson," said Florry, gaily. "I'm quite healthy."

"Ah, yes, now," replied Mr. Spolger, darkly, sitting down; "but that thin dress means a chill. It might settle on the lungs, and you might be in your coffin before you know where you are."

"Nonsense, man," said Marson, in a hearty voice; "the room is quite warm. Won't you take off that heavy coat?"

"Not at present," answered Mr. Spolger, emphatically. "I always accustom myself to the temperature of a place by degrees. A sudden chill is worse than damp feet."

"Will you have some tea, Mr. Spolger?" asked Judith, for the footman had now brought in the teapot and a plate of toast.

"No, thank you," answered the hypochondriac, politely. "I'm undergoing a course of medicine just now, and tea in my present condition means death."

"Then have some toast," said Florry, laughingly, presenting him with the plate.

"Buttered," said Mr. Spolger, looking at the plate. "Horrible! The worst thing in the world for me! I take dry toast for breakfast, with a glass of hot water—nothing more."

"I hope you don't intend me to breakfast like that," said Florry, saucily.

"My dear, you can eat what you like," answered Mr. Spolger, solemnly producing his little book. "Should you suffer from your indiscretion, I have always got the remedy in this."

"Did the medicine Dr. Japix prescribed do you good?" asked Judith.

"Not a bit," said Spolger, slowly taking off his coat. "I still suffer from sleeplessness. However, I've got a new idea I'm going to carry out. Cold water bandages at the head, and a hot brick at the feet. There, now my coat is off I feel beautiful."

"Well! well!" said Mr. Marson, rather impatient of all this medical talk, "I hope you'll be quite well for your wedding."

"I hope so, too," retorted Spolger, with gloomy foreboding. "I've arranged all the tour, Florry. We go first to Malvern, a very healthy place, then to Bath to drink the waters. After that, if you like, we'll go abroad, though I much distrust the drainage of these foreign towns."

"Oh, let us go abroad at once," said Florry, eagerly; "to Paris. If you find it too lively, you can walk everyday in the Père-la-Chaise Cemetery."

"Don't jest on such a subject, Florry," said Judith, reprovingly.

"Oh, I don't mind," replied the lover, with gloomy relish; "we'll all have to go to the cemetery some day, so it's as well to get accustomed to the idea."

His three listeners looked rather depressed at this dismal prophecy, but said nothing, while Mr. Spolger told cheerful little stories of how his liver would treat him if he did not look after it. This led him to talk of medicine, which suggested chemists, which in their turn suggested Wosk & Co., so by-and-by Mr. Spolger began to talk of Monsieur Judas.

"A most estimable young man," he said, feeling his own pulse in a professional manner; "he has had typhoid fever twice, and suffers from corns."

"Tight boots?" asked Florry, flippantly.

"No, hereditary! Most curious case. But talking of Monsieur Guinaud—"

"Judas," said Miss Varlins, smiling.

"Yes, I hear they call him Judas on account of his red hair," replied Mr. Spolger, laughing carefully. "Well, as a chemist, he takes a great interest in Florry."

"In me?" cried the damsel, indignantly.

"Yes; he thinks you look delicate," said Mr. Spolger, complacently; "indeed, he suggested several remedies. And if you would see him—"

"No, no!" interposed Marson, quickly. "Really, Jackson, I'm astonished at you. If Florry requires to see a medical man, there is Dr. Japix; but as to letting a man like that Frenchman meddle with her health—why, the very look of him is enough."

"Consumption," said Mr. Spolger, sagaciously; "he looks delicate, I know."

"I think he is a very dangerous man," said Judith, in her quiet, composed voice; "he was a great friend of—" Here she checked herself suddenly.

"Of Melstane," finished Spolger, scowling. "Yes, I know that. And talking about Mr. Melstane—"

"Don't talk about Mr. Melstane," said Marson, sharply.

"Why not?"

Florry answered him, for she was evidently struggling with a fit of hysteria, and as he spoke she arose from her seat and fled rapidly from the room, followed by Judith.

"There," said Marson, in an annoyed tone, "how foolish you are to speak of that scamp!"

"I don't see why Florry shouldn't get used to his name," replied Spolger, sulkily. "Of course, I know she loved him, but it's all over now; he won't trouble her again."

"Why not?" demanded Marson, quickly.

"Because he's gone away. He had the impudence to call on me before he went, but I soon settled him, though he upset me dreadfully."

"What did he call about?"

Spolger was going to reply, when once more the door was thrown open, and the footman announced in stentorian tones:

"Mr. Roger Axton."

"Oh, how do you do, Mr. Axton?" said Mr. Marson, going forward to meet the young man. "I did not know you were down here."

"No! I came by this morning's train from town," replied Roger, shaking the old man's hand. "I trust you are well, Mr. Spolger?"

That gentleman shook his head as Axton sat down, and lights being brought in at this moment, looked sharply at the new-comer, answering his question in the Socratian fashion by asking another.

"Are you well?"

"Oh, yes!" replied Roger, hurriedly, "perfectly. I suffer a good deal from sleeplessness."

"You should try—"

"Spolger's Soother, I suppose?"

"No," said Jackson, solemnly, "I never recommend that to my friends. You should try morphia. Why, what's the matter?"

"Nothing," answered Roger, faintly, for he had started violently at the mention of the drug, "only I'm rather nervous."

"You've been overworking, I suppose," said Mr. Marson, looking at him keenly; "burning the midnight oil."

"No, indeed! I've been on a walking tour."

"Very healthy exercise," said Mr. Spolger, approvingly. "I can't indulge in it myself because I've a tendency to varicose veins. What part of the country were you walking in?"

"Down Winchester way," replied Roger, raising his eyes suddenly and looking at Mr. Marson steadily.

"Oh, indeed!" answered that gentleman, with a start; "then I suppose you were near Jarlchester."

"I was at Jarlchester," said Roger, emphatically, "during the investigation of that case."

Both his listeners were silent, as if some nameless fear paralysed their tongues; then Marson looked at Spolger, and

Spolger looked at Marson, while Roger glanced rapidly from one to the other.

At this moment Judith entered the room.

"Florry is better," she said, advancing; "she is— What, Mr. Axton!"

"Yes; I came down here to see a friend, and thought I would look in," replied Roger as she greeted him.

"I am very glad you did not forget us," she remarked, quietly resuming her seat. "Will you have a cup of tea?"

"Thank you!"

They were seated beside the tea-table, and were quite alone, as Mr. Marson in company with his future son-in-law had left their seats, and were now talking together in low whispers at the end of the room. Judith handed a cup of tea to Roger, and looked at him steadily as he stirred it with a listless expression on his worn face.

"You don't look well," she said at length, dropping her eyes.

"Mental worry," he responded, with a sigh. "I have undergone a good deal since I last saw you."

"In connection with that?" she asked, in a low voice.

"Yes! I received your letter in London, and went at once down to Jarlchester on a walking tour, that is, I made my walking tour an excuse for being there. I stayed there a week, and then received your second letter saying he was coming."

"And he came?" asked Judith, with a quick indrawn breath.

"He did."

"You saw him?" she continued, looking nervously towards the two whispering figures at the end of the room.

"Yes!"

"And got—and got the letters?"

"Of course," said Axton, in a tone of surprise. "I sent them to you—to the post office, as you desired."

"My God!" she said, in a low voice of agony, "I—I have not received them. I went to the post office every day to ask for a packet directed to Miss Judith, but have been told it had not come."

"Good heavens!" said Roger, with a start of surprise, "I hope they have not gone astray—I ought to have registered them."

"If you had I could not have obtained them," replied Miss Varlins, hurriedly; "you forget. The packet was addressed to Miss Judith, and the postmistress knows me so well, I could not have signed any but my own name without causing remark."

"You ought to have allowed me to send them here."

"Yes! and then Florry would have seen them."

"Nonsense!"

"There is always a possibility," said Judith, quickly; "but if these letters have gone astray, what are we to do?"

"Well, if—"

"Hush!"

She laid her hand suddenly on his arm to arrest his speech, for at that moment the voice, thin and peevish, of Mr. Spolger, was heard saying a name:

"Sebastian Melstane."

Judith and Roger both looked at one another, their cheeks pale, their manners agitated, and he was about to speak again when she stopped him for the second time.

"Listen!"

They could hear quite plainly, for the pair at the end of the room had moved unthinkingly near them, and Spolger was talking shrilly to Mr. Marson about the man of whom they were then thinking.

"He came up to see me before he went away. I was very ill, but he would see me, and we had a most agitating interview. Told me that he loved Florry—told me, her affianced husband. Said that she would never marry me— that he could prevent the marriage. Then he insulted me. Yes! held out a box of pills, and asked me if I had any ideas beyond such things. I knocked the box out of his hand and insisted upon his leaving the house. He went, for I was firm —very firm though much agitated. He left the box behind him. Yes, I found it after he was gone, and sent my servant down with it to his boarding-house. Oh, I was terribly agitated. He was so bold. But he won't come back again. No! he won't come back."

"How do you know that?" cried Roger, starting to his feet, in spite of Judith's warning touch.

"What! you were listening," said Mr. Spolger, angrily,

115

coming near to the young man.

"I could hardly help hearing you, seeing you raised your voice," retorted Roger, sharply.

"Most dishonourable! most dishonourable!"

"Sir!"

"Gentlemen! gentlemen!" said Francis Marson, plainly, "you are in my house."

"I beg your pardon, Mr. Marson," said Roger, ceremoniously, "I only asked Mr. Spolger a simple question."

"To which he declines to reply," replied Mr. Spolger, coolly.

"Why?"

Judith had risen to her feet and was clinging to Francis Marson's arm, while Roger and Spolger looked steadily at one another. The whole four of them were so intent upon the conversation that they did not see a little figure enter the door and pause on the threshold at the sound of the angry voices.

"You agitate me," said the valetudinarian, angrily. "I am not used to be agitated, sir. I was telling my friend a private story, and you should not have listened.

"I apologise," replied Roger, bowing. "I did not intend to give offence, but I wondered how it was you guessed Melstane would never return."

The little figure stole nearer.

"What do you mean?" asked Spolger, quickly.

Judith leaned on Marson's arm with her face deadly white and her eyes dilated, waiting—waiting for what she dreaded to think.

"I mean about the Jarlchester Mystery."

Mr. Marson said nothing, but with a face as pale as that of the woman on his arm, stared steadily at Roger Axton. At the mention of Jarlchester the figure behind came slowly along until Florry Marson, with a look of terror on her face, stood still as a statue behind her lover.

"I have read in the papers about the Jarlchester Mystery," said Spolger, in an altered tone.

"I guessed as much, and that was the reason you said Melstane would not return."

"No, no! What do you mean?"

"Mean that Sebastian Melstane died at Jarlchester, and you know it."

"Sebastian!"

They all turned round, and there stood Florry, with one hand clasped over her heart, and the other grasping a chair to steady herself by.

"Sebastian," she whispered, with white lips, "is—is he dead?"

Roger turned his head.

"Dead!" she cried, with a cry of terror. "Dead—murdered!" and fell fainting on the floor.

Chapter 9

A Terrible Suspicion

Eight o'clock in the evening by the remarkably incorrect clock on the mantelpiece, eight-thirty by Mr. Fanks' watch, which was never wrong, and that gentleman was seated in a private room of the "Foundryman Hotel" waiting the arrival of Roger Axton.

The "Foundryman" was not a first-class hotel, nor was the private room a first-class apartment, but it was comfortable enough, and Mr. Fanks was too much worried in his own mind to pay much attention to his personal wants. He was much disturbed about his old schoolfellow, as everything now seemed to point to Axton as a possible murderer—the conversation at Jarlchester, the evidence of Dr. Japix, the delicately insinuated suspicions of Judas—it seemed as though no doubt could exist but that Roger Axton was the person responsible for the death of Sebastian Melstane.

In spite, however, of all this circumstantial evidence, the detective hoped against hope, and resolved within his own honest heart not to believe Roger guilty until he had heard his explanation of the affair. He knew well that circumstantial evidence was not always to be depended upon, and Axton's prompt arrival in answer to his letter had inspired him with the belief that the young man must be innocent, otherwise he would hardly dare to place himself in a position of such peril. So Mr. Fanks, with the perplexity of his mind showing even in his usually

118

impassive face, sat watch in hand, awaiting Roger's arrival and casting absent glances round the room.

A comfortable room enough in an old-fashioned way! All the furniture seemed to have been made at that primeval period when Ironfields was a village, but here and there some meretricious hotel decoration spoiled the effect of the whole. Heavy mahogany arm-chairs, a heavy mahogany table, a heavy mahogany sideboard stood on a gaudy carpet with a dingy white ground, and sprawling red roses mixed with painfully green leaves. An antique carved mantelpiece, all Cupids and flowers and foliage, but on it a staring square mirror with an ornate gilt frame swathed in yellow gauze, and in front of this a gimcrack French timepiece, with an aggressively loud tick, vividly painted vases of coarse china containing tawdry paper flowers, and two ragged fans of peacock's feathers. The curtains of the one window were drawn, a cheerful fire burned under the antique mantelpiece with its modern barbarisms, and an evil-smelling lamp, with a dull, yellow flame, illuminated the apartment. Mr. Fanks himself sat in a grandfatherly armchair drawn close to the fire, and pondered over the curious aspect of affairs, while the rain outside swept down the crooked street, and the wind howled at the window as if it wanted to get in to the comfortable warmth out of the damp cold.

A knock at the door disturbed the sombre meditations of Octavius, and in response to his answer, Roger walked into the room with a flushed face and a somewhat nervous manner. He did not attempt to shake hands (feeling he had no right to do so until he had explained his previous behaviour at Jarlchester), but sat down near the fire, opposite to his friend, and looked rather defiantly at the impassive face of that gentleman, who gave him a cool nod.

119

"Well," he said, at length, breaking a somewhat awkward silence, "I've lost no time in answering your letter."

"I'm glad of that, Roger," responded Fanks, gravely; "it gives me great hopes."

"How? That I'm not a criminal, I suppose."

Fanks said nothing, but looked sadly at the suspicious face of the young man.

"Silence gives consent, I see," said Axton, throwing himself back in his chair, with a harsh laugh. "Well, I'm sorry a man I thought my friend should think so ill of me."

"What else can I think, Roger?"

"He calls me Roger," said Axton, with an effort at gaiety. "Why not the prisoner at the bar—the convict in the jail—the secret poisoner?"

"Because I believe you to be none of the three, my friend," replied Fanks, candidly.

Roger looked at him with a sudden flush of shame, and involuntarily held out his hand, but drew it back quickly, before the other could clasp it.

"No, not yet," he said, hastily; "I will not clasp your hand in friendship until I clear myself in your eyes. You demand an explanation. Well, I am here to give it."

"I am glad of that," replied Fanks for the second time. "I'm quite aware," continued Roger, flushing, "that now you are at Ironfields you must be aware that I concealed certain facts in my conversation with you."

"Yes! You said you had not been to Ironfields, and that you

did not correspond with Miss Varlins. Both statements were false."

"May I ask on whose authority you speak so confidently?" demanded Axton, coldly.

"Certainly. On the authority of Dr. Japix."

"Japix!" repeated Roger, starting, "do you know him?"

"Yes! I met him some time ago in Manchester, and I renewed my acquaintance with him down here."

"Why?"

"Because I wanted him to analyse those pills found in Melstane's room after his death."

He looked sharply at Roger as he spoke, but that young man met his gaze serenely and without flinching, which seemed to give Fanks great satisfaction, for he withdrew his eyes with a sigh of relief.

"Octavius," said Roger, after a pause, "do you remember our conversation at Jarlchester?"

Mr. Fanks deliberately produced his secretive little note-book and tapped it delicately with his long fingers.

"The conversation is set down here."

"Oh," said Roger, with sardonic politeness. "I was not aware you carried your detective principles so far as to take a note of interviews with your friends."

"I don't do it as a rule," responded Fanks, coolly; "but I had an instinct that our interview might be useful in connection with Melstane's case. I was right, you see. Roger," he cried, with a burst of natural feeling, "why did you not trust me?"

Roger turned away his face, upon which burned a flush of shame.

"Because I was afraid," he replied, in a low voice.

"Of being accused of the murder?"

"Yes!"

"But you can exculpate yourself?" said Fanks, in a startled tone.

"I hope so," replied Roger, gloomily; "but on my word of honour, Fanks, I am innocent. Have you read 'Edwin Drood'?"

"Yes!" responded Fanks, rather puzzled at what appeared to be an irrelevant question, "several times."

"Do you remember what Dickens says in that novel?" said Axton, slowly. "'Circumstances may accumulate so strongly even against an innocent man that, directed, sharpened, and pointed, they may slay him.'"

"True, true," answered Fanks, approvingly nodding his head; "such things have occurred before."

"And may occur again," cried Axton, with a look of apprehension. "I know that you suspect me; I know that circumstantial evidence could be brought against me which would put my life in danger; but on my soul, Fanks, I am innocent of Melstane's death."

"I feel certain you are," answered Octavius, gently; "but, as you say, circumstances are strong against you. Tell me everything without reserve, and I may be able to advise you; otherwise, I am completely in the dark."

"I believe you are my friend, Fanks," said Roger, earnestly. "I believe you know me too well to think I would be guilty of such a dreadful crime. Yes; I will tell you everything, and place myself unreservedly in your hands. But first tell me how it is you are so sure it was murder and not suicide!"

"Certainly! It is well we should both be on common ground for the better understanding of your explanation. Regarding the death of this Melstane, I own that at Jarlchester I was half inclined to believe in the suicide theory, and had it not been for the name Ironfields on that pill-box, which gave me a clue, would probably have acquiesced in the verdict of the jury. Following up the clue, however, I went to the chemists, Wosk & Co.'s, where the pills were made up, and discovered that originally there were twelve in the box. I could account for the disposal of six, so that ought to have left a balance of half-a-dozen."

"True! but if I remember, when I counted them at Jarlchester there were eight."

"Exactly! Two extra pills were placed in that box by some unknown person whom I believe to be the murderer of Melstane."

"Why?"

"Because I took the pills to Dr. Japix, and he analysed the whole eight; seven were harmless tonic pills, the eighth compounded of deadly morphia."

"What!" cried Roger, starting to his feet, "and Melstane died of morphia!"

"He did! Now do you understand? The murderer, whoever

he was, placed two morphia pills sufficient to cause death in the box. Melstane took one in complete innocence and died, the other was analysed by Japix and found to contain sufficient morphia to kill two men."

"It's wonderful how you have worked it out," said Roger, with hearty admiration; "but how do you connect me with the murder?"

"I did not say I connected you with the murder," replied Fanks, hastily; "I only said there were suspicious circumstances against you. For instance, you had morphia pills in your possession."

"How do you know that?" asked Roger, with a start of surprise.

"Japix told me."

"Yes, and Japix prescribed them," cried Axton, starting to his feet. "I own that does look suspicious; but I can set your mind at rest on that point. Will you permit me to withdraw for a moment?"

"Don't talk nonsense, Roger," said Fanks, angrily; "of course I will."

Axton said nothing, but left the room, leaving Fanks considerably puzzled as to the cause of his departure. In a few minutes, however, he returned and placed in the detective's hands a box of pills.

"There," he said, resuming his seat, "if you count those pills you will find there are eleven. The original number was twelve; I only took one, and finding it did me no good, left the rest in the box. Am I correct?"

"You are," replied Fanks, who had counted the pills; "there are eleven here."

"If you have any further doubts, you can ask Wosk & Co., who made up the pills."

"There is no need. I believe you."

"But I would prefer your doing so," said Roger, urgently.

"Very well," replied Fanks, calmly putting the box in his pocket; "I will see about it to-morrow. But now you have set my mind at rest on this point, and I have told you my story, tell me yours."

Roger paled a little at this request, and remained silent for a few moments.

"Fanks," he said at last, with great solemnity, "you have your suspicions of me now, and perhaps when I tell you all, you may consider them to be confirmed. What then?"

"What then?" echoed Fanks, cheerfully. "Simply this. Knowing your character as I do, I don't believe you would be guilty of a cold-blooded murder, so when you tell me your story we will put our heads together and try to find out the true criminal."

"I'll be only too glad to do that," said Roger, gratefully, "if only to regain your confidence which I have lost."

"Well, go on with your story."

"I told you a good deal of it at Jarlchester," replied Axton, looking at the fire thoughtfully; "but I will reveal now what I concealed then. The first time I met Judith Varlins was in this town. I came down with letters of introduction from a London friend to Mr. Marson, and he made me free of his house—in fact, he wanted me to stay there; but though I am poor I am proud, so preferred to put up at Binter's Boarding-house."

"Yes, I know that place."

"How so?"

"I went there to see a Monsieur Guinaud."

"Then you saw an uncommonly good specimen of a scoundrel. He was a great friend of Melstane's, and they both hated me like poison. I don't know why Judas—that's his nickname here—did, but Melstane had a grudge against me because I put a stop to his secret meetings with Florry Marson by telling Judith."

"Why did you do that?"

"Because Melstane was such an out-and-out scoundrel that I did not want him to marry that silly little thing. If he had done so, he would have broken her heart. Well, when Judith became aware of these meetings, she took Florry off to Ventnor. I escorted them to London, where they stayed for a time, and then went on to the Isle of Wight. Shortly afterwards I followed them. I told you all that took place there. On our return to Ironfields about the middle of October, I believed Melstane met Florry by stealth, and I taxed him with it. We had a furious row, and I went off to London. While there I received a letter from Miss Varlins, telling me that Florry was engaged to Mr. Spolger, and that Melstane was leaving Ironfields for Jarlchester."

"How did she know that?" asked Fanks, sharply.

"I don't know; perhaps Florry told her. She, of course, could easily learn it from her lover; but what puzzles me is why

126

Melstane went to Jarlchester at all."

"You have no idea?" said Octavius, looking at him keenly.

"Not the least in the world. I'm quite at sea as to his reasons."

"Humph! Go on!"

"Judith asked me to go to Jarlchester and await the arrival of Melstane, in order to obtain from him a packet of letters written by Florry, which he had in his possession."

"Yes," said Fanks, eagerly; "go on!"

"I went down to Jarlchester ostensibly on a walking tour, and received a second letter from Judith, telling me Melstane had left Ironfields, and was on his way down. On the day he was expected to arrive, I went for a walk, intending to return early. Unfortunately, however, I lost my way and did not get back until late at night. I found Melstane had arrived and gone to bed."

"Did you ask if Mr. Melstane had arrived?"

"No! I asked casually if a stranger had arrived, and they told me one had come from London, and described him, so of course I knew him at once."

"But why all this mystery?"

"Judith implored me to be careful," said Roger, quickly. "You see Florry's good name was at stake, and I wanted to get the packet of letters back with as little publicity as possible."

"Nevertheless, you rather overdid the mystery business! Well, what did you do when you found Melstane had gone to bed?"

"I went to bed also, and made up my mind to see him the next morning. Thinking of the letters, however, and knowing he was in the next room, I could not sleep, so as it was not then twelve o'clock, I thought I would go in and see him."

"Curious thing to make a visit to a man's room at that time."

"I dare say," replied Axton, tartly; "but you see, I was anxious to get the letters, and knowing that Melstane was a nervous man, particularly at night, I fancied I might get them back by playing on his fears."

"A most original idea!"

"Rather wild, perhaps, but not without merit. Well, I put on my things, took my candle, and went into his room."

"Ho! ho! so it was you that left the door ajar!"

"It was. I went into the room quietly, and saw he was sound asleep. On the table near the bed was a bundle of letters which he had evidently been reading."

"How did you know it was the bundle you wanted?"

"Because I recognised Miss Marson's writing on the top letter."

"Well, seeing that was the bundle you were in search of, what did you do?"

"Rather a mean thing—I stole them."

"Stole them! Upon my word, Roger, you are a nice young man!"

"In fighting with a man like Melstane, I had to make use of his own weapons," retorted Roger, coolly. "It seems dishonourable to you for me to go into a man's room and steal a bundle of letters; but I was dealing with a scoundrel; those letters contained the honour of a young and inexperienced girl whom he held at his mercy. If I had awakened him there would have been a row, he would have raised the alarm, and I would have got into trouble, so I did the best thing—the only thing to be done under the circumstances and stole the letters."

"Did you see the pill-box when you were in the room?"

"No, I was in such a hurry to go, having once secured what I wanted, that I did not stop to look at anything, but went back to my room."

"Leaving the door of No. 37 ajar," said Fanks, reprovingly, "foolish man."

"Ah! you see I was not experienced in midnight burglaries."

"Well, after you got back to your own room, what did you do?"

"I went to bed and slept soundly. Next morning I sent the packet of letters to Judith, and went off on a stroll. When I came back at night, I was horrified to learn Sebastian Melstane was dead. The rest you know."

"When you spoke to me, did you really and truly believe he had committed suicide?"

"Yes, I did," replied Roger, honestly. "I thought he had found out the loss of the letters, and seeing that his hold over Florry Marson was lost, had committed suicide in desperation."

"How did you account for the morphia?"

"I didn't attempt to account for it. All I knew was that I had secured the letters, that Melstane was dead, and that Florry was safe."

"So that's all. I wish you had told me all this at Jarlchester."

"I tell you I was afraid to do so. Look how black the case appears against me. I fight with a man here; I follow him down to Jarlchester; I have morphia pills in my possession; I go into his room at night, and in the morning he is found dead of morphia. Why, if I had told all this, I would have been arrested. Florry's name would have come up. That infernal Monsieur Judas would have put his spoke in, and I would very probably have been hanged on circumstantial evidence."

"I don't wonder you were afraid," replied Octavius, thoughtfully; "but seeing I was your friend, you might just as well have trusted me."

"You are a detective."

"I am your old schoolfellow."

"Then you believe I am innocent?"

"I do. If you were guilty, you would not have told a story so dead against yourself."

"Will you shake hands, then?" asked Roger, colouring and holding out his hand.

"By all means," replied Fanks, solemnly, and the two friends shook hands with honest fervour.

"Now, then," said Octavius, when this ceremony was

concluded, "the next thing to be done is to find out who killed Melstane."

"It's an impossibility," cried Roger, in despair.

"No, I don't say that," answered Fanks, coolly. "At Jarlchester I had nothing to go upon, and yet look what I've discovered."

"You are a genius, Octavius."

"Egad! I've need to be to unravel this case," said Octavius, smiling. "It's the most difficult affair I ever took in hand."

"Do you suspect any one?"

"I can't say at present till I get things more in order. The first thing I want to know is, what were the contents of those letters?"

"I cannot tell you. I did not read them, of course, but simply packed them up and sent them to Miss Varlins."

"Oh, then she has got them?"

"No, she hasn't."

"Where are they, then?"

"Lost."

"Lost How so?"

"I can't tell you," said Roger, helplessly. "You see, Miss Varlins did not want them sent to the Hall, as Florry Marson might have got hold of them, and if she had, she's such a little fool, and was so much in love with Melstane, that she probably would have sent them straight back."

"Well, as they did not go to the Hall, where did they go?"

"To the post office in this place. The postmistress, however, knows Miss Varlins, and had the packet been addressed in that name, would have sent them up at once to the Hall. To make things safe, however, I directed the letters to Miss Judith, Post Office, Suburban Ironfields, and she was to call for them."

"I suppose she called?"

"Yes, every day, but the postmistress said no packet had arrived."

"Strange! The postal arrangements are very good as a rule. Letters don't often go astray. Addressed to Miss Judith, you say?"

"Yes."

Fanks pinched his chin thoughtfully between his finger and thumb, looked frowningly at the fire, and then looked up suddenly:

"Is the postmistress here intelligent?"

"No, the reverse. A snuffy old idiot."

"Oh!" said Fanks, smiling to himself; "then I wouldn't be surprised if she had delivered that packet to the wrong person."

"But there's no one else about here called Judith."

Mr. Fanks did not reply, but leaving his chair, went to the sideboard and brought back pen, ink, and paper, which he placed on the table near Roger.

"You're a very bad writer!" he said, calmly arranging the paper.

"No worse than the usual run of literary men."

"I'm sorry for the printers, if that is the case. The letter you sent me here, saying you were coming, is most illegible."

"Well, that letter has nothing to do with the case," said Roger, impatiently.

"I think it has a good deal to do with it, seeing it told me you were coming down here," replied Fanks, coolly. "However, this is not to the point. Take up that pen." Roger did so, looking considerably bewildered at the manner in which his friend was behaving.

"Now write me down the address you put on the packet." Axton obeyed quickly, and produced the following scrawl:

"Miss Judith, Post Office, Suburban Ironfields"

"Humph!" said Fanks, looking at this specimen of caligraphy. "Most careless writing. Observe; you use the old-fashioned 's.' You don't dot your 'i's,' nor cross your 't's,' and, moreover, you curve your 'i' towards the next letter in the fashion of 'a.' So far so good. Now write M. Judas."

Roger did so with no idea of what his friend had in his mind.

"There," observed Fanks, when this was completed, "do you see much difference between Judith and Judas, according to your writing?"

"No," said Roger, honestly, looking at them, "I can't say that I do. But what do you mean?"

"I mean that the postmistress—old and stupid, as you say she is—has made a mistake, and delivered the packet to Monsieur Judas."

"Absurd!"

"Not at all. Judith Varlins is generally called Miss Varlins, I presume, so the Christian name Judith would not occur to this old woman. On the other hand, the odd name Judas would, and knowing that extraordinary-looking Frenchman to be called Judas, she—I mean the postmistress —would naturally hand the packet over to him."

"But surely he would refuse to receive it?"

"I don't know so much about that. In the first place, he might have thought the packet was for him, and in the second, his natural curiosity would make him take it home to examine. When he found what the packet contained, he kept it."

"But why should he keep it?"

"How dense you are, Roger!" said Fanks, irritably. "He was a friend of Melstane's, and seeing the letters were addressed to Melstane, he very likely kept them by him to return to his brother scamp."

"Then you think Monsieur Judas has the packet?"

"I'm certain of it. We'll call and see what we can do to-morrow."

"All right; but why are you so anxious to get the packet?"

"For several reasons. I believe that packet to contain letters to Melstane, not only from Miss Marson, but from her father also; and I further believe," continued Fanks, sinking his voice to a whisper, "that in that packet is contained the secret of Melstane's death."

"But you surely don't suspect Mr. Marson?" cried Roger, aghast.

Octavius rolled up the paper upon which Roger had been writing and threw it into the fire as he answered, with marked emphasis on the latter part of his reply:

"I suspect no one—at present."

Extracts From A Detective's Note-Book

". . . I feel much more at ease now I have seen Roger . . . He has explained away my suspicions . . . It is true that his story tells very much against him, but to my mind this fact assures me of his innocence, as no guilty man would tell a story so much against himself . . . Yes, I am sure he is not guilty . . . He acted foolishly in obeying Miss Varlins' instructions—in keeping the truth from me at Jarlchester . . . . Nevertheless, his conduct has not been that of a guilty man, and whosoever poisoned Sebastian Melstane, it was certainly not Roger Axton . . .

". . . I am much troubled about the disappearance of those letters, and would like to see them . . . There must be something in them which may throw light on this mysterious affair . . . I have no grounds for declaring this, but I think so . . . If Mr. Marson, who did not want his daughter to marry Melstane, wrote, his letters must be in

136

that packet . . . It is his letters I wish to see . . . Now, however, by the unfortunate mistake of the postmistress, the letters are in the possession of Judas . . . This again implicates him in the affair . . . I don't like the attitude of Judas at all . . . Could he—but no, it's impossible; he has no motive . . . Sebastian Melstane was his friend, so there was no reason he should wish him out of the way . . . I believe that Judas holds the letters in order to make capital out of them with Mr. Marson . . . I'll thwart him on the point, however . . .

"*Mem.*—To see the postmistress to-morrow and find out for certain if the packet was delivered—as I verily believe—to Judas."

Chapter 10

The Missing Letters

Suburban Ironfields being, as has been stated, a poor relation of the opulent city, fared badly enough in all respects, after the fashion of all poor relations. Every comfort, every luxury, every improvement pertaining to nineteenth century civilisation was to be found in Ironfields itself; but the quondam village from whence it had sprung retained many of its primitive barbarisms.

This was especially the case with the post office, a low-roofed, dingy little house squeezed into an odd corner of the crooked main street, and presided over by an elderly lady named Mrs. Wevelspoke and her son Abraham. Ironfields magnates—dwellers in the palatial residences beyond the village—received their correspondence straight from the prompt, businesslike office of the city itself; but this unhappy little town depended for the transmission and delivery of its letters on old Mrs. Wevelspoke and her snail-footed son.

Many complaints had been made about the disgraceful way in which this place was conducted; but as the complainants were mostly poor people, no attention was paid to their remonstrances, and Mrs. Wevelspoke and her son went on in their own quiet way, delivering letters late, delivering them to the wrong people, and very often not delivering them at all.

The postmistress herself was a snuffy old woman of great antiquity, with a shrivelled face, two dull eyes like those of a dead codfish, a toothless mouth, and a wisp of straggling gray hair generally hidden under a dingy black straw bonnet with rusty velvet trimmings; she wore a doubtfully black gown, which had acquired a greenish tinge from great age, a tartan shawl of faded colours pinned over her bony shoulders, and rusty mittens on her skinny hands. She always wore her bonnet—it was her badge, her symbol, her sign of authority; and although, perhaps, she did not, as scandal averred, sleep in it all night, she certainly wore it all day. She was deaf, too, and spoke to other people in a shrill, loud voice, like a querulous wind, as if she thought, as she did, that they suffered from the same infirmity. She was also doubtful as to her powers of vision, so it can easily be seen that the Suburban Ironfielders had good ground for complaint against her. As to Abraham, he was a dull-looking youth, who thought of nothing but eating, and only delivered the letters because walking gave him an appetite for his meals. He never hurried himself, and at the present moment was deliberating as to whether he would then take the letters in his hand to their recipients, or let them wait until the afternoon.

"Now then, Abraham," piped Mrs. Wevelspoke, viciously, "ain't you gone yet?"

"You see I ain't," growled Abraham, in a fat voice.

"Don't say you won't go," said his mother, shrilly, "'cause you've got to earn bread and butter. Not that it's good, for that baker's failin' off awful, and as to the butter, it ain't got nothin' to do with the cows, I'm certin. But bread and butter's butter an' bread, so git out and git it."

"I'm goin', I'm goin'!" grumbled Abraham, slowly, putting on his hat, "but I ain't well, mar, I ain't. That corfee's a-repeatin' of itself like 'istory, an' the h'eggs weren't fresh! Poach 'em, fry 'em, or biled, they taste of the chicken."

"Pickin'," said Mrs. Wevelspoke, giving her rusty bonnet a hitch, "pickin' up the letters, which you don't do, Abraham. Do 'urry, there's a good boy. Mrs. Wosk is waitin' for that blue un—a bill, maybe—and Mr. Manks is gettin' noos of 'is son from Australy in that thin paper un, an' there's Drip and Pank and Wolf all waitin' to 'ear the 'nocker, so lose no time, my deary."

"It's all right as I don't lose no letters, mar," retorted Abraham, going to the door. "I'm orf, I am, mar. I'll be back by six, mar, and do see arter the tripe yourself; it don't agree overcooked."

When Abraham had departed, his parent busied herself with sorting the letters and newspapers into their respective pigeon-holes, communing with herself aloud as she glanced at the addresses on each.

"Drat 'em!" she said, alluding to the writers of the letters. "Where's their eddication, as they don't write plain? If I were a Board School, which I ain't, I'd school-board 'em, with their curly 'p's' and 'q's,' as like pigs' tails as ever was, to say nothin' of leavin' the 'i's' and 't's' undone for want of dottin'. 'Ow do they expect 'em to be delivered straight wen I ain't no scholard to read their alphabets?"

"Mrs. Wevelspoke," said a full, rich voice proceeding from a lady on the outside of the counter.

"P-h'o-h's-t," spelt Mrs. Wevelspoke, slowly, not hearing that she was called, and not seeing that any one was present by reason of her back being turned; "that spells post, but it don't look like one. M.—that's for Mary, I dare say; M. J-u-h'l-e-h's; ho, it's for that Judas thing at Wosk's. If 'is name's Judas, why do he call himself G-u—"

"Mrs. Wevelspoke," repeated the lady, rapping her umbrella on the counter quickly, "is that letter for me?" The postmistress, having a faint idea that she heard some distant noise, turned round slowly, and saw Miss Varlins leaning forward with an eager look on her face.

"Is that letter for me?" she repeated, pointing to the envelope still in Mrs. Wevelspoke's hand.

"This un?" said Mrs. Wevelspoke, seeing by the gesture what was meant. "Oh dear, no, Miss Varlins. Your name ain't Mary—nor July, I take it."

"But it's Judith."

"What?" asked Mrs. Wevelspoke, deafly.

140

"Judith," said Miss Varlins, very loudly.

"Oh, your fust name, miss. You speak so muddled like, mum, as I can't make out your 'ollerin', miss. But if your fust name's Judith, mum, your last ain't—ain't G-u-i-h'n-h'a-u-d."

"Mrs. Wevelspoke, let me look at the letter, please," cried Judith, impatiently, taking the envelope from the old woman. "I can tell you if it's for me in a moment."

It certainly was not for her, as the direction was plain enough:

> "M. Jules Guinaud
> c/o Wosk & Co.,
> Chemists,
> Suburban Ironfields."

"No, it's not for me," said Miss Varlins, handing it back reluctantly with a sigh of regret. "But are you sure you have no packet addressed to Miss Judith?"

"It ain't for her," said Mrs. Wevelspoke, putting the Frenchman's letter into the pigeon-hole marked "J." "You want a letter, I s'pose, miss?"

"Yes."

"There ain't no Varlins," said Mrs. Wevelspoke, after a cursory glance at the "V's". "No, miss, your letters is all sent to the 'All."

"This letter I want was addressed to Miss Judith, and would not be sent to the Hall."

"To 'Judas'?" said Mrs. Wevelspoke, catching the name wrongly. "Ho, his letters go to the shop, mum."

"I thought as much," remarked a quiet voice behind Miss Varlins, as she turned to find herself face to face with the speaker and Roger Axton.

"We've been listening, Miss Varlins," explained Roger, hastily, as she shook hands with him. Then seeing the startled look on her face, he went on hurriedly: "I can explain the reason, but first let me introduce Mr. Rixton, a friend of mine."

Judith bowed coldly, and waited for Roger's promised explanation, which was to be given by the gentleman called Mr. Rixton.

"Allow me, my dear Roger," he said, genially. "The fact is, Miss Varlins, my friend here told me about this packet of letters addressed to you as 'Miss Judith,' and I put forward a theory accounting for their non-delivery, so Mr. Axton and myself came here to see if my theory was correct."

"But what is your theory?" asked Judith, rather bewildered.

"That the letters were delivered by that old woman to Monsieur Judas, instead of to you."

"But Judas is a nickname," said Miss Varlins, quickly; "all his letters would be addressed to Monsieur Guinaud."

"Quite correct," replied Octavius, quietly, "but with such an unintelligent postmistress mistakes are sure to occur. I'm pretty certain she delivered the packet to our red-headed friend, and I'm going to try to find out. You posted the packet at Jarlchester on the 13th of this month, did you not, Roger?"

"Yes; on the morning of the 13th."

"Then it would get to London late in the afternoon, and go

on to Ironfields at once. I should think it would be ready for delivering here about midday on the 15th. Did you call here on the 15th, Miss Varlins?"

"No; I did not expect the packet so soon. But I came next day."

"Too late, I'm afraid," said Octavius, advancing to the counter. "Here, old lady. Was there a letter here on the 15th, directed to Miss Judith?"

"Judas!" replied Mrs. Wevelspoke for the second time. "Drat it, what's come to the man, sir, as you're all talkin' of him? He's at Wosk's if you want him."

"Did you send any letters to him this month?" asked Fanks, loudly.

"Letters! all his letters go to the shop," retorted Mrs. Wevelspoke, obstinately.

"Were there any this month—November?"

"Remember!" cried the postmistress, twitching her bonnet, "of course I remember—I can remember things afore you were born, young man. I sends all letters to Mr. Judas at the shop. Two this month, and there's another waitin' 'im."

"Let me see it!" said Fanks, quickly glancing at Roger, "it may reveal something, Miss Varlins."

"Steal," remarked Mrs. Wevelspoke, sharply. "No, you don't steal here, sir! I'm an honest woman, I am."

"And a very stupid one," said Fanks, ruefully, in despair at getting any information out of this old dame.

"I have seen the letter she talks about, Mr. Rixton," said Miss

143

Varlins, quickly, "and it is not the one we want."

At this moment Abraham rolled into the office, and Fanks at once pounced on him as being more likely to give information than his superior.

"Oh, here's the postman," he cried, radiantly. "Here, postman, did you deliver a letter to Monsieur Guinaud at Wosk's shop about the beginning of this month?"

"I can't tell State secrets," said Abraham in his fat voice, "it's treesin."

"Oh, you won't come to Tower Hill for telling me this," replied Fanks, good-humouredly.

"I don't know nothin' about your Tower Hills," growled the portly one, sulkily, "but I ain't going to tell nothin', I ain't. Mother and me's sworn, we are."

Fanks did not want his true occupation to be known, but he saw perfectly well that he would get nothing out of the faithful Abraham unless he adopted strong measures, so he made up his mind how to act at once.

"Look here, my man," he said, taking Abraham to one side and speaking sharply. "I'm a detective, and you must give me a plain answer to a plain question."

"I ain't bin doin' nothin' wrong," whimpered Abraham, edging away from the representative of the law; "I'll tell you anythin' you like as long as it isn't State secrets."

"This isn't a State secret," said Fanks, quickly, putting a half-a-crown into the lad's fat hand; "just tell me if you delivered a thick packet to Monsieur Guinaud on the 15th of this month?"

The faithful servant of the State was not proof against bribery, so he answered at once:

"Yes, sir, I did! Only the letter was to Monsieur Judas."

"Not to Miss Judith?"

"Lor, sir, I don't know; mother said it were Monsieur Judas, and as there's only one Judas here, I took it to him."

"At Wosk & Co.?"

"Yes, sir."

"Did he take it?"

"Yes, sir."

"Very well, that will do," said Fanks, in a gratified tone; "now hold your tongue and say nothing to nobody."

"But mother, sir!"

"Not even to your mother. If you told her, all the town would hear, she's so deaf."

So Abraham the faithful grinned, and slipping his half-a-crown into his pocket, retired, while Fanks went outside, where he found Judith seated in her carriage and Roger talking to her.

"It is as I thought," said Octavius, anticipating their questions; "the postman told me he delivered the packet to Judas."

Judith uttered an exclamation of horror, upon hearing which the detective glanced sharply at her.

"Are you afraid of Judas seeing those letters?" he asked,

quickly.

Miss Varlins passed her handkerchief across her dry lips, and after a pause answered with great deliberation, showing thereby how strong was her self-control.

"I don't know anything of the man," she said, quickly, "beyond that he was a friend of Mr. Melstane; but that in itself is sufficient to make me anxious. The letters contain nothing more than the usual romantic nonsense a girl would write. At the same time, knowing this Frenchman to be, as I verily believe, an unscrupulous wretch, I am afraid he may use the letters for his own ends."

"But what can he gain by showing them," said Fanks, sagaciously, "seeing they contain nothing of importance?"

He spoke with such pointed significance and emphasis that Judith, fiery-tempered by nature, flashed out suddenly with great spirit.

"I don't know how much Mr. Axton has told you, sir, but I question your right to speak to me in this manner."

"Oh, Fanks doesn't mean anything," interposed Roger, unthinkingly.

"Fanks!" cried Judith, with a start, looking at Octavius, "I thought your name was Rixton?"

"My real name is Rixton," said Fanks, glancing reproachfully at Roger, "but I use the name of Octavius Fanks—"

"For your detective business," finished Judith, coolly. "Oh, you need not look surprised, sir. I have read the Jarlchester Mystery, and I know you have the case in hand."

"If that is so, perhaps you will help me in the matter?"

146

"I—I cannot help you," she said, faintly, again passing the handkerchief over her lips.

"You can in one way," said Fanks, quietly.

She looked at him sharply, but unable to read anything on his impassive countenance, threw herself back in the carriage with an uneasy laugh.

"How so?"

"By letting me read those letters now in the possession of Judas."

"No!"

She said it so firmly that both Fanks and Axton glanced at her in surprise, upon which she leaned forward with a pale face, and spoke hurriedly.

"There is nothing—really nothing in those letters beyond foolish girlish talk; I assure you, Mr. Rixton, there is nothing at all."

"Then why refuse to let me see them?" asked Octavius, quickly.

"They are private."

"Not when the law desires to see them. I am the law, and I intend to see those letters."

"What do you mean, Fanks?" said Roger, angrily, indignant at this tone being used to Miss Varlins.

"What I say," responded Fanks, coolly. "Axton, Miss Varlins, this case is in my hands, and I am determined to find out

147

who killed Sebastian Melstane, and for reasons of my own I wish to see those letters. Will you let me look at them?"

Judith twisted her handkerchief in her gloved hands evidently trying to control herself, then putting up one hand to her throat, gave a hysterical laugh.

"Yes, on one condition.

"And that condition?"

"That you let me look over them before you read them."

The detective fixed his hawk-like eyes on her face, as if he would drag the meaning of the words from her unwilling lips, but she gave no sign likely to guide him, and seeing that he had to deal with a will as iron as his own, compromised the matter.

"You can look over them," he said, calmly, "in my presence."

Roger Axton turned furiously on his friend.

"How dare you insult Miss Varlins?" he said, fiercely. "Are you a gentleman?"

"I am a detective," replied Fanks, significantly.

"There is no need to quarrel, gentlemen," said Judith, quietly. "I agree to Mr. Rixton's request. If you will both get into the carriage we can drive to Wosk's, obtain the letters, and settle Mr. Rixton's doubts at once."

Fanks bowed in silence, and stepped into the carriage without further remark, but Roger turned sullenly away. "Thank you, I prefer not to come," he said, stiffly.

"I want you to come, please," observed Fanks, quietly. Roger did not reply, but looked at Judith, who made him an almost imperceptible sign, upon which he sprang in without further objection, and the carriage went on to the chemist's at once. Octavius had noticed the sign, and wondered thereat, but like a wise man said nothing.

"I can afford to wait," he thought, rapidly; "but I wish I saw the end of this case. I'm afraid of what I may find out."

At the door of the shop of Wosk & Co. they all alighted, and Miss Varlins, followed by the two men, entered. Judas came forward as they stood by the counter, and on seeing his visitors narrowed his eyes down at once to their most dangerous expression.

"Humph!" thought Fanks, grimly, "Judas knows our errand."

"Monsieur Guinaud," said Judith, calmly, "there was a packet directed to Miss Judith at the post office here, which, I learn, was delivered to you by mistake. May I ask you to return it to me?"

Judas shot a glance of amazement at Fanks, with whom he credited this tracking of the letters, and opening his crafty eyes to their widest, looked guilelessly at the lady.

"Mais oui, mademoiselle," he said, with a shrug, "de lettres you do tell me of are with me. C'est bien certain ze postage was mistook. Mais why to you I gif zem?"

"Because the packet was meant for me."

"Yes; I posted it," said Roger, quickly. "It was given to you by mistake."

"It is de name 'Mademoiselle Judith," observed Guinaud,

149

doubtfully.

"Which was how the mistake occurred," explained Fanks, easily. "Come, Monsieur Guinaud, hand over those letters at once, if you please."

"Eh, très-bien," answered Judas, promptly. "I haf no wis to them keep. Zey are nosing to me. I did not know ze person zey were to."

"Well, you know now," cried Fanks, sharply. "Please give them to this lady without delay."

"Mais certainement," replied the Frenchman, with a bow. "Pardon, monsieur."

He retired quickly, and in a few minutes returned with the packet of letters—open.

"Have you read these?" cried Judith, indignantly, as she took the packet.

Monsieur Judas smiled in a deprecating manner, and shook his head.

"I am a man of the honour, mademoiselle," he said with great dignity, "an' I haf not read ze lettres. I tawt de lettres pour moi, and I did open zem. But wen I do zee zem in anglais I see it is mistook, an' read zem not."

Fanks kept his eyes on Judas as he spoke, to see if he was speaking the truth, but was quite unable to arrive at any decision, so calm was the Frenchman's voice, so immobile the expression of his face.

"Well, at all events we have got the letters," he said to Miss Varlins. "And now—"

"Now you can take them home to read," replied Miss Varlins, contemptuously, tossing the packet to him.

"But are you not going to examine them?"

"I have done so."

"Are all the letters there?"

"Monsieur," cried Judas, "do you tink—"

"I'm addressing Miss Varlins," retorted Fanks, coldly. "Are all the letters there, Miss Varlins?"

"Yes, I think so," she replied, with faint hesitation.

"You are not sure?"

"As sure as I can be," she replied, keeping her temper wonderfully. "I think they are all there. Will you please read the letters, and then return them to me?"

"Certainly."

"Thank you. Good morning," replied Judith, coldly. "Mr. Axton."

Roger bowed and conducted her to the carriage, while Fanks, with the bundle of letters in his hands, stood looking after her in an irresolute manner.

Suddenly he felt a cold touch on his hand, and turned round to see Judas looking at him with a strange smile on his crafty face.

"You are afraid," he said, in French.

"Of what?" answered Fanks, coldly.

"Of those," pointing to the letters; "of her," indicating Judith; "of him," nodding in the direction of Roger; "of all. You are afraid, monsieur, of what you may discover."

Fanks looked steadily at him, made no reply, and walked quickly out of the shop.

Chapter 11

No Smoke Without Fire

This is the episode of Mr. Spolger, which came about in this wise. Roger was very indignant with his friend for speaking so plainly to Judith, and told him so in somewhat strong language when the carriage had departed. Fanks said nothing at first, being much exercised in his own mind over the peculiar attitude taken up towards him by Miss Varlins, but Axton was so very free in his condemnations, that for the moment he lost his self-control, and answered sharply.

"I've taken up this case, Roger, and I intend to carry it out to the bitter end, if only for your sake; but you must let me act in every way as I think best, otherwise—"

"Otherwise!" repeated Axton, angrily, as Octavius paused.

"I will throw up the whole affair."

"No, you must not do that," said Roger, quickly. "I want to see the end of this for my own sake, as you very truly say,

152

so don't leave me in the lurch for the sake of a few hasty words. But you must admit, old fellow, that you spoke rather sharply to Judith."

The philosophic Fanks thereupon recovered his temper and said sententiously:

"Women are the devil."

"Eh, how so?"

"They cause trouble whenever they get mixed up in any affair. This case was difficult yesterday; to-day it is more difficult because feminine influence is now at work."

"With whom?"

"With me, with you, with Judas, with us all. May I say something without being thought rude?"

"If it's about Judith—"

"It is about Judith."

"Then don't say it," retorted Roger, in a huff.

"Very well," replied Fanks, resignedly; "but if you take away my guiding stars I'll never find my way across the ocean of mystery."

Roger made no reply, but walked on rapidly with a frown on his good-looking face. Suddenly he stopped so dead short that Fanks, also using his legs in no slow fashion, shot past him a yard or so before he could pull up.

Quoth Roger savagely:

"Say your say and have done with it."

Mr. Fanks surveyed his friend with a quiet smile, and then took him gently by the arm.

"Come and have luncheon with me," he said, persuasively.

"No."

"They've got an excellent cook at the 'Foundryman.'"

"I won't come."

"I can give you a good bottle of claret."

Axton exploded furiously.

"Confound it, Fanks, why do you treat me like a child?"

"Because you are one at present."

"Oh, indeed," said Roger, with a sneer, "from your point of view."

"From a common-sense point of view," replied Fanks, with great good-humour. "Come, don't be silly, my good fellow! You're sore because I don't worship your idol. Be easy, I'll do so when this case is finished."

"But if—"

"Oh, come to luncheon," said Fanks, and marched him off without further parley.

The luncheon was good, both as regards victuals and wine, while Fanks, in the capacity of host, behaved in a wondrously genial fashion, so by the time they finished and were smoking socially by the fire, Roger had quite recovered his temper, and felt ashamed of his fit of ill-humour.

"But you know," he said, guiltily, "I'm in love."

"Business first, pleasure afterwards," quoth the philosopher, sagely.

"Apropos of what?"

"This case. I know you are in love, I know the lady you love. I quite approve of that love. Marriage, however, should begin with no secrets between man and wife."

"Pish!"

"In this case the wife would have a secret from the husband."

"Rubbish!"

"It may be, but it's rubbish that concerns those letters."

"Perhaps you'll accuse Judith of the murder," cried Roger, in great wrath.

A blank wall would have been more expressive than the face of the detective.

"Why didn't she want me to read those letters?" he asked, quietly.

"There are the letters—read them."

"Thank you," replied Fanks, imperturbably, "I will." And he did so slowly and carefully, taking note of the dates and arranging the letters in due order. Having finished, he tied the letters up again and handed them over to Roger.

"Please deliver them to Miss Judith."

"Oh, ho," said Roger, slipping the parcel into his pocket. "So the letters are no use to you?"

155

"Not the letters that are there."

"What, do you think some of the letters are missing?"

"I'm certain of it."

"Then who is the thief?"

"Judas."

"Oh!"

Roger flung himself back in his chair with a sigh of relief, as if he had half expected to hear another name, and that a name similar in sound.

"There are in that bundle," said Fanks, gravely, "letters written at Ironfields—so far so good. But they are only silly girlish letters!"

"As Judith told you!"

"Exactly, as Judith told me," responded Octavius, suavely, "but I want to see the letters written in London and in Ventnor."

"Perhaps she never wrote any in those two places."

"Humph! the chances are she did."

"You are excessively mysterious," said Roger, sarcastically, "but the question can easily be settled. Ask Miss Marson herself."

"I thought I heard Miss Varlins say she was ill!"

"So she is, poor child," said Roger, soberly; "I blurted out the fact of Melstane's death too suddenly, and she fainted. Now she is very ill."

"Oh! brain fever?"

"I'm afraid so!"

"In that case I can get nothing out of her," said Fanks, coolly; "it's a pity. By the way, do you know who I think knows a good deal about this case?"

"Monsieur Judas."

"You'll make a good detective some day," replied Fanks, approvingly. "Yes! I mean Monsieur Judas. He's a crafty wretch, that same Frenchman, and knows a good deal."

"About Melstane and Miss Marson?"

"Probably."

"And Melstane's death?"

"Possibly."

"You don't suspect him?" asked Roger, breathlessly.

"I don't suspect any one—at present, as I said before," replied Fanks, with a sudden movement of irritation. "Confound it, the more I go into this case the more mixed up it seems to get. It seems to me it all depends on those pills. The box went from Wosk's shop into the hands of Melstane, certainly—"

"Yes, and it went from Melstane's hands into those of Spolger," said Axton, with sudden recollection.

"What do you mean?" asked Fanks, eagerly.

Whereupon, Roger, in a terrible state of excitement, told his friend all about Melstane's interview with Spolger—of the pill-box left behind, and of the sending of it back to Melstane.

"And don't you see, Fanks," cried Axton, in great excitement, "Spolger is a bit of a chemist, so he could easily put in the two extra pills before he sent back the box. Melstane would never suspect, and so would come by his death. Oh, Spolger's the man who killed Melstane, I'm certain of it."

"Wait a bit," said Fanks, rapidly making a few notes in his pocket-book. "When a crime is committed, the first thing is to look for a motive. Now, what motive had Spolger for killing Melstane?"

"Motive!" repeated Roger, in amazement, "the strongest of all motives. He was in love with Florry and wanted to marry her. She, however, was in love with Melstane, and while he lived Spolger had no chance. So of course he removed his rival by death. It's as clear as daylight."

"Why! 'of course'?" said the detective, putting his note-book in his pocket. "Even love would hardly make a man like Spolger commit a crime."

"He's a scoundrel."

"Eh! but a nervous one."

"He's fond of Florry."

"And fond of his own skin."

"I tell you I'm convinced he committed the crime."

"Don't jump to conclusions."

"I'm not jumping to conclusions," retorted Axton, hotly.

"Look at the case, you blind bat. Spolger loves—adores Florry. He wants to marry her, but finds out she won't have him because she loves another man. Chance, by means of the forgotten pill-box, throws in his way the means of injuring that other man. What is more natural? He takes advantage of the chance."

"Injuring a man doesn't mean killing him."

"Who said it did? Put it in this way. Spolger intended to merely injure him, but in making up the morphia pills he puts in too much of the drug, and kills Melstane without intending to do so."

"Theory! Pure theory!"

"Well, as far as I can see, the case is all pure theory at present."

"By no means. We have ascertained the cause of death; the way in which the drug was taken; also a number of suspicious circumstances connected with Melstane's past life. That's not all theory."

"I think the most suspicious theory connected with Melstane's past life is Monsieur Jules Guinaud, better known as Judas."

"Because he has red hair and a crafty face," said Fanks, coolly.

"No; because he loves Florry."

"How do you know?"

"I think so."

"Ah, that's theory," replied Fanks, nodding his head; "purely theoretical, if you like. Well, we must be off."

"Where to?"

"To test your theory. I'm going to see Mr. Jackson Spolger."

"He'll tell you nothing," said Axton, putting on his coat.

"Perhaps not; but his face may. He's a nervous man. Japix told me that, so if he knows anything about this murder, he may betray himself unconsciously. Come along."

So they went down into the sloppy street and hired a cab, but just as they were going to step in, Fanks suddenly darted to the window of a brougham standing a short distance away. It was a large brougham, and contained a large man, who put out his head when he saw Fanks, and roared out a welcome in a stentorian voice:

"Hey, Monsieur Fouché!"

"Don't advertise me so publicly, Japix."

"Pooh! no one here knows Fouché. They think he's a Chinese."

"It's best to be on the safe side, anyhow."

"Very well, Mr. Rixton."

"That's better. I say, Doctor, do you believe in patent medicines?"

"No," roared Japix, indignantly, "I don't."

"But I've been advised to take Spolger's Soother."

"Then don't take it. Who advised you?"

"A lady."

"Humph! Only a woman would give such silly advice. If you're ill, come to me like Spolger, and I'll cure you, but don't touch his medicine."

"Is it dangerous?"

"Not very. The pills are only bread, gum, and morphia."

"Morphia?"

"Yes; small quantity, of course. Not like that pill you gave me to analyse the other day. Good heavens!" exclaimed Japix, as a sudden idea struck him, "what do you mean?"

"I'll tell you to-night."

"When you come to dinner?"

"Yes; can I bring Axton with me?"

"By all means. Good day!"

"Good day!" replied Fanks, and darted back to his cab, where he found Roger awaiting him.

"Roger," he said, when the vehicle started towards the Spolger residence, "there may be something in that idea of yours after all."

"I think so. But why do you say that?"

"Because I've just discovered that Spolger puts morphia in his pills."

Chapter 12

The Spolger Soother

The residence of Mr. Spolger, situate about a mile beyond the town, was a large and particularly ugly building constructed on strictly hygienic principles. The inventor of the "Soother" had lived in an ancient mansion, badly drained and badly ventilated, which had been erected many years before; but when his son entered in possession of his inheritance, he had pulled down the old house, and built a barrack-like structure in which beauty gave way entirely to utility. Square, aggressively square, with walls of glaring white stone, it stood in the midst of a large piece of ground perfectly denuded of trees, as Mr. Spolger deemed trees damp and unhealthy, so the bare space was gravelled and asphalted like a barrack-yard. Plenty of staring plate-glass windows admitted light into the interior, which was composed of lofty square rooms, lofty oblong corridors, all smoothly whitewashed.

The floors of polished wood, innocent of carpets, were dangerous to the unwary, and the furniture, all of solid oak, was made for strength rather than loveliness. There were few pictures on the walls, as Mr. Spolger thought that looking at works of art strained the optic nerve, and there were no draperies on the windows in case any disease might lurk in them. The bare inside looked out on to the bare barrack ground, and the treeless barrack ground looked into the glaring inside, so it was all very nice and healthy and abominably ugly.

In the midst of this fairy-like creation sat the proprietor thereof, by a hot-air stove, wrapped in a woollen dressing-gown, and engaged in measuring out his daily drops. A respectful manservant, wrinkled like a snake, and black-clothed like a rook, stood beside Mr. Spolger with a small printed form of directions, which he was reading for his master's information, with regard to the effects of the drops. The servant, Gimp by name, was moist about the eyes, a fact which suggested drink, and he read the dull little pamphlet in a subdued whisper which was pleasant to the ears of the valetudinarian.

"The effect of these drops," droned Gimp, with a weary sigh, for the pamphlet was by no means exciting, "is to raise the spirits. Mrs. Mopps, of Whitechapel, who suffered from rheumatics engendered by her daily occupation of charing, was advised to try them by a humble friend who had been cured by them of liver complaint. Mrs. Mopps did so, and took four drops daily in a wine-glassful of gin. She is now cured—"

"Ah!" said Spolger, with great satisfaction, "she is now cured."

"And doesn't suffer more than three days a week," finished Gimp, in a depressed tone.

"Oh, she's not quite cured, then," observed his master, regretfully; "it must have been the gin. Gin is so very bad."

"Very bad, sir," replied Gimp, like a parrot.

"It makes the eyes moist."

Mr. Gimp closed his own eyes tightly, aware that they betrayed him; but his master was too busy with his own ailments to trouble about the looks of any one else, and went on carefully with his measuring.

"Eight," he said, handing the bottle back to Gimp, "I think that will do for a beginning. How many diseases does it cure, did you say?"

"Seven," said Gimp, drearily; "liver, rheumatism, headache, bed sores, nerves, consumption, and delirious trimmings."

"Quite an all-round medicine. I've got a liver, and I often have a headache. I had rheumatism the winter before last; my nerves, of course, I always have. Bed sores? No, I've not had bed sores—yet."

"Not been in bed long enough, sir, I think," hinted Gimp, respectfully.

"No, quite right; but I may come to it. Consumption? Well, you know, Gimp, I'm not quite sure of my lung? What's the last?"

"Delirious trimmings, sir."

"I've not had that—I don't think I ever will have it; drink is death to me. I hope these drops will do me good. Give me the water, please. Ah, there that's right. Now!"

IIe drank off the mixture slowly, with the air of a connoisseur, and gave the empty glass to the servant.

"Not much taste, Gimp. No; I've tasted nastier. Put the glass away, please. Have you heard how Miss Marson is to-day?"

"Just the same, sir. Delirious."

"Ah! how terrible! I wonder if those drops would do her good?"

"I think not, sir," said Gimp, drifting towards the door; "it's 'er 'ead, ain't it, sir, not drink?"

"Yes, yes! You're quite right, Gimp. I must go over and see her again; and the day's so damp. Oh, dear, dear! Close the door, please, there's such a draught."

Gimp did as he was told, and retreated noiselessly from the room, after which Mr. Spolger went over all his ailments in his own mind to make sure that he had forgotten none of them, examined his tongue in the mirror, felt his pulse carefully, and having thus ministered to his own selfishness, gave a thought to the lady he was engaged to.

"Poor Florry!" he moaned thoughtfully, "how she must have loved that man, and he wasn't healthy. I'm sure there was consumption in his family. I wonder if she loves me as much. Ah, that faint was such a shock to my nerves; so unexpected. I'd had pins and needles in the left leg. That is the first sign of paralysis. Oh, I do hope I'm not going to get paralysis."

This idea so alarmed him that he arose hastily to see if his limbs would support him, and fell back in his chair with a subdued shriek as the shrill tones of an electric bell rang through the room.

"The front-door bell," he said, peevishly. "Oh, my nerves! I must really have the sound softened. I wonder who wants to see me. I won't be seen. Who is it?"

This question was addressed to Mr. Gimp, who had entered the room in his usual stealthy manner, and now handed his master two cards.

"Mr. Roger Axton and Mr. Octavius Fanks," read Spolger, slowly. "I can't see them, Gimp, I really can't. The action of the drops demands perfect quiet."

"The gentlemen have druv from town, sir."

"Well, they must just drive back again," said his master, crossly. "My compliments, Gimp, and I'm too ill to see them."

Gimp obediently retreated, but shortly afterwards returned with a curt message.

"Mr. Axton ses he must see you, sir."

"Oh, dear, dear!" moaned Spolger, irritably, "those healthy people have no consideration for an invalid. Well, if I must, Gimp, I must. But I see them under protest. Let them understand distinctly—under protest."

Gimp once more disappeared, and on his reappearance ushered in Axton and Fanks, whom Mr. Spolger received with peevish politeness.

"I'm sorry I kept you waiting, gentlemen," he said, waving his hand, "but my health, you know. I'm a mere wreck. I don't want to be jarred on. Pray be seated! Mr. Axton, you don't look well. Mr.—Mr.—"

"Fanks," said that gentleman, introducing himself, "Octavius Fanks, detective."

"Oh, indeed," replied Spolger, starting, "a detective, eh! I think I've seen your name in the papers lately."

"Yes," said Axton, bluntly, "in connection with the Jarlchester affair."

"Oh, indeed," repeated their host once more; "suicide, I believe, although Mr. Melstane did look consumptive. I incline to the latter. Now which idea do you favour, Mr.

Fanks—suicide or consumption?"

"Neither! It was a case of murder."

"Murder!"

Mr. Spolger jumped up in his chair as if he had been shot, and his face turned a chalky white.

"Pooh pooh!" he said at length, with an attempt at jocularity, "absurd, monstrous! The jury said suicide."

"I'm aware of that," responded Fanks, coolly, "but I don't agree with the jury. Sebastian Melstane was murdered."

"By whom?"

"That's the mystery."

Spolger said nothing, but wriggled uneasily in his chair under the somewhat embarrassing gaze of his visitors, and at length burst out into feeble protests against their candour.

"Why do you speak to me like this? I don't know anything about murders. They upset my nerves. I'm quite unstrung with all I've come through. What with Miss Marson's illness, and Melstane's death, and all kind of things, I'm quite uneasy in my mind."

"What about?" asked Fanks, sharply.

"I've mentioned what about," retorted Spolger, tartly. "I wish you would go away."

"So we will when you've answered our questions."

"I won't answer any questions."

"Oh, yes, you will. It will be wiser for you to do so."

"I—I—don't understand," stammered Spolger, feebly.

"Then I'll explain," said Fanks, composedly. "Melstane died from taking a morphia pill, which was placed in a box of tonic pills by some unknown person."

"And what's that got to do with me?"

"Everything," said Axton, suddenly speaking. "Remember the story you told at Mr. Marson's the other day. You had the box of tonic pills in your possession for a time, and—"

"Oh," interrupted Spolger, very indignantly. "And I suppose you'll say that I put the morphia pill into the box in order to kill Melstane!"

"That's the idea," said Fanks, coolly.

"A very ridiculous one."

"I don't see it. You did not like Melstane, because he was loved by Miss Marson. You use morphia for your 'Soother,' so what was to prevent your acting as you suggest?"

"Don't—don't!" cried Spolger, putting out his shaking hands with a sudden movement of terror. "You'll argue the rope round my neck before I can defend myself. I did not like Melstane, certainly, but I had not the slightest idea of killing him. I'll swear it."

Fanks suddenly arose to his feet, and walked across the room to a shelf whereon were displayed a number of drugs in glass bottles. The invalid had risen to his feet, and was looking steadily at him, while Axton, similarly fascinated by Fanks' actions, leaned forward to see what he was doing.

The detective's hand hovered lightly over the array of bottles, then suddenly swooped down with the swiftness of a hawk upon one which he bore to the table. It was a large glass bottle half filled with a white powder, and labelled "Morphia."

"There!" he said, as he placed it before Spolger, triumphantly.

"I know that bottle. But what has that to do with this murder?"

"Melstane died from morphia."

"It's no good going over the old ground," said Spolger, with a scowl. "I can easily prove my innocence. Please touch that bell, Mr. Axton."

Roger did so, whereupon a shrill sound rang through the house, and Mr. Spolger dropped back into his chair with an expression of acute suffering on his face. Then Gimp made his appearance with such marvellous rapidity that it was quite plain that he must have been listening outside the door, but he walked into the room with the utmost composure, and waited to be addressed.

"Gimp," said his master, sharply, "do you remember the day Mr. Melstane called?"

"I do, sir."

"Do you remember what took place?"

"Certainly, sir."

"Then tell these gentlemen all about it."

Gimp at once addressed himself to Fanks, who stood by the table with one hand on the jar of morphia and the other in his pocket, looking at the servant to see if he was speaking the truth.

"Mr. Melstane called, sir," said the respectable Gimp, deliberately, "a few weeks ago to see my master. He saw him, and I believe, sir, they had words."

Spolger nodded his head to affirm that such was the case. "I was called in, sir, to show Mr. Melstane out. I did so, and he swore awful."

"And after you showed Mr. Melstane out?"

"I came back, sir, to this room, and found my master much agitated—nerves, I think, sir."

"Yes; a bad attack!"

"My master pointed to a pill-box on the floor, and told me to run after Mr. Melstane with it. I did so, but could not see him, so I took the pill-box down to Mr. Melstane's lodgings that evening."

"The pill-box was in your possession the whole time?"

"Yes, sir! It was wrapped in white paper, and sealed with red wax, sir. I didn't know it was a pill-box till master told me."

"And I knew it was, because Melstane held it out to me and asked me if I made pills like that," said Spolger, savagely. "Well, Mr. Axton, I hope you are satisfied."

"Perfectly," said Fanks, with great politeness; "but please tell me, when did you use this morphia last?"

"Not for months," replied Spolger; "the pills are made at the factory, and I never trouble about them. I don't know if you've noticed it, sir, in your desire to make out a case against me, but that bottle is tied with string across the stopper and sealed."

"Ah! that's the very thing I'm coming to. The seal is broken."

"Impossible!" cried Spolger, coming to the table to examine the bottle; "I haven't used it for a long time, and sealed it when I last used it! Gimp, how is this?"

"I'm sure I don't know, sir; the bottle ain't been touched to my knowledge."

"Does any one else come into this room?"

"None of the servants," said Spolger, after a pause;

"Gimp looks after everything here."

"Oh! what about your visitors?"

"Well, now and then I see some one here—just like yourselves."

There was a faint hesitation in his tone, which Fanks was quick to detect, and which prompted his next question: "Has Mr. Marson been in here?"

"Often!"

"And Miss Varlins?"

"Oh, yes! both the ladies have been here; but they would not touch any of my drugs. They know how particular I am."

Fanks said nothing, but remained for a time in meditative silence, which Spolger broke by asking him if he would take some refreshment.

"No, thank you," he replied, quickly. "I'm much obliged to you, sir, for your courtesy. Are you ready, Roger?"

"Oh, yes, I'm coming," said Axton, rising to his feet. "Have you heard how Miss Marson is to-day, Spolger?"

"Just the same, I believe."

"Poor girl!"

"Yes, it's dreadful!" responded Spolger, with a groan; "of course the marriage will have to be put off. I'm not sorry, because I'm so upset. Fancy being taken for a murderer!"

"Oh! not as bad as that," said Fanks, good-naturedly; "I only thought you might throw some light on the mysterious affair."

"Well, I can't," said Spolger, curtly.

"No; I see that. Good day, sir."

"Good day," replied their host, with a bow. "I hope you'll be successful in your search for the real criminal."

Fanks made no reply, as he had his own idea regarding Mr. Spolger's good wishes, but departed, followed by Axton; the last thing they heard being the voice of the invalid complaining about the door being left open.

When they were seated in their cab and once more on their way to Ironfields, Fanks broke the silence first.

"Roger, it was a mare's nest after all."

"Yes; he knows nothing."

172

"I'm not so sure about that."

"Do you mean to say he is concealing something?"

"I don't know what to say," said Fanks, testily, "but I think some one else is concealing something."

"Whom do you mean?"

"You'll be angry if I tell you."

"No, I won't. Who is it?"

"Judith Varlins!"

Extracts From A Detectives Note-Book

". . . It is as I thought . . . The packet was delivered to Judas . . . We (Roger and myself) met Miss Varlins by chance and had a very strange interview with her . . . She did not want me to look at the letters . . . I got my own way at last, when the packet was delivered by Judas . . . She looked at the letters, and I saw an expression of great relief on her face . . .

"Query. Could she have written to Jarlchester to Melstane? . . . Were there any letters there likely to implicate her in the crime? . . .

". . . If so, those letters, I think, have been stolen, and by Judas . . . However, I can't tell for certain . . . I looked over those letters and found nothing . . . Strange! Query, What does Miss Varlins mean by this strange conduct? . . .

". . . Roger told me a queer story about Spolger concerning

the pill-box . . . We went up to see Spolger, but the whole affair turned out to be a mare's nest . . . All my suspicions now point to Judith Varlins . . .

". . . Spolger and Axton have both proved their innocence of the crime.

". . . Query. What about Miss Varlins?. . ."

Chapter 13

The Craft of Monsieur Judas

There was no doubt that Florry Marson was dangerously ill, for the sudden shock she had sustained in hearing of the unexpected death of Melstane had unsettled her brain. Weak, shallow, and frivolous, she was not the woman to stand bravely against calamity, and this first great sorrow of her life had rendered her completely prostrate. The poor butterfly which had rejoiced in the sunshine of prosperity was now lying on a bed of sickness, whence it seemed doubtful that she would ever rise. Through the long hours she lay helpless on her back, babbling incoherently of her past life, or else fought furiously with Judith to leave her bed, and go on imaginary errands; while her cousin, a patient and untiring nurse, never left her side. She loved Florry as a mother loves a wayward child, and although she was bitterly disappointed by the duplicity of which her darling had been guilty with regard to Melstane, yet she could not find it in her heart to be seriously angry with this poor, weak nature now broken down by a dangerous illness.

In truth, it was a very melancholy house, for while Judith sat in the sick-room watching the patient, Francis Marson was pacing to and fro in his study, wondering what would be the end of all this trouble. One thing he saw clearly, that unless he could obtain a large sum of ready money he would be a ruined man in a very short space of time. Relying on the promises of Jackson Spolger, he had thought he would be able to tide over the commercial depression now existing in Ironfields; but now that Florry was ill the marriage could not take place, and his future son-in-law absolutely refused to do anything to aid him. Unless his daughter recovered and married Spolger, he could expect no help from that quarter, and not knowing where else to turn for assistance, ruin, swift and irretrievable, would be the end.

To and fro he paced with bowed head, revolving in his weary brain a thousand schemes, all of which he rejected as chimerical as soon as they were formed. With that curious noting of trivial things habitual to overtaxed and over-worried brains, he mechanically marked the pattern of the carpet and planted each footstep directly in the centre of each square, counting the number with weary precision as he blindly groped for a way out of his difficulties.

"Spolger won't do anything. Five! six! No! he's too selfish, and unless the marriage takes place I can expect no help from him—fourteen squares from that wall. All those bills are due in three months, and unless I can meet them there is nothing left but bankruptcy. I'll count back again. One! two! three! So the house of Marson & Sons must go down after all, and Florry, poor child, how ill she is! I'm afraid she will not recover. Ten! ten! Ah, if I only had ten thousand, that would help me. Twenty, twenty-one! How my head aches! Who's that? Come in, Judith!"

It was indeed Judith who stood on the threshold of the room, looking pale and ghost-like in her white dressing-gown, with her long black hair loose over her shoulders. She held a candle in her hand, and the yellow light flared on her strongly marked features, ivory white under the shadow of her hair.

Francis Marson stood by his writing-table in the circle of light which welled from under the green shade of the lamp, but he made a step forward as Judith entered slowly and closed the door after her with great care.

"Is Florry worse?" asked Marson, with a look of despair on his haggard features.

"No! just the same," replied Judith, placing the candle on the table and sinking into a chair. "Dr. Japix says she will be like she is now for some time—until the crisis comes."

"And then?"

Judith let her head fall on her breast.

"I don't know," she said, in a monotonous voice; "it means either madness or sanity."

"Better she should die."

"Yes, I think so," answered Judith, with terrible calmness. "Poor Florry, she was so bright and happy a few days ago, and now her life is spoilt; she will never be the same again."

"And all through that cursed Melstane."

"Yes!"

There was silence for a few moments, and Marson sank slowly into his chair, shading his worn face with his thin left hand, while the other mechanically busied itself with two pens lying on the table. Judith, with her hands lying loosely clasped on her lap, stared straight in front of her with a thoughtful expression, as if she was engaged in solving some abstruse problem.

Only the steady ticking of the clock, the subdued crackling of the dying fire, and shadows everywhere! In the corners of the room, overhead on the ceiling, where the bright glare of the study lamp made an unsteady circle, on the faces of the man and woman—shadows everywhere, and, darkest of all, the shadow intangible, unseen, the shadow of horror, of guilt, of disgrace that hung over the whole splendid mansion!

"Are you going to see him to-night?"

It was Judith who spoke with sharp interrogation, and Marson lifted his head wearily as he said:

"Guinaud?"

"Yes."

"I must see him. He wrote to me that he had to speak upon a matter of importance, and I promised to grant him an interview."

"What time did he say he would be here?"

"Between seven and eight o'clock to-night."

With a simultaneous impulse they both looked at the clock. It was half-past seven.

"He will be here shortly," said Judith, looking at Mr. Marson.

"I presume so."

"Don't see him."

Marson raised his head quickly, and flashed a keen glance at her eager face.

"I beg your pardon, Judith?"

"Don't see him."

"I must."

Judith drummed with her fingers on the table, an anxious look appeared in her splendid eyes, and she frowned angrily. Marson saw all the signs of a coming storm, and waited. He had not long to wait.

"That man is a scoundrel," burst out Judith, in sombre fury; "he is coming here to tell you a lot of lies."

"How do you know?"

"I'm certain of it. He was a great friend of Sebastian Melstane's—a treacherous, cowardly friend, who played the traitor to his friendship."

"How so?"

"Because he loves Florry."

"Impossible!"

"It's true, I tell you," said Judith, doggedly; "he knew Mr. Melstane loved Florry, but that did not deter him from

178

loving her himself. He has shown by a thousand signs that he loves her, and he kept it from no one but his dead friend. Oh, he's not called Judas for nothing."

"I don't see what all this has to do with the interview."

Judith sprang to her feet, and crossing over to the table laid her hand lightly on his shoulder. He shrank from that light touch, but otherwise gave no sign of emotion.

"Do you know why he is coming here to-night?" she hissed into his ear. "Do you know what he intends to ask you? No, I see you don't! He is coming here to tell you something —something that is dangerous to you, and must be kept secret. He is coming to ask his price—that price is the hand of your daughter."

Marson looked at her in surprise as she towered above him, and he was about to speak, when a knock came to the door. Without waiting for an invitation to enter, a servant appeared with a card on a salver. He held out the salver to his master, but Judith picked up the card lying thereon and read it.

"Monsieur Jules Guinaud! Show him in here, Marks!"

The servant bowed and retired, while Marson looked suddenly at Miss Varlins.

"Are you going to wait?"

"Not here," she said, pointing to a door masked by curtains at the end of the room; "I am going into the next room."

"To listen?"

"No! I am going upstairs to put on my dress, and will then come down and hear what Monsieur Guinaud has to say."

"He wants the interview to be a private one."

"Do you?"

Marson did not answer, but sat nervously plucking at his chin.

"You are dealing with a dangerous man," she said in a whisper, not knowing how near Judas might be to the door; "he needs a woman to deal with him. Hush! there is Guinaud! I'll go upstairs this way and be back shortly. Not a word."

She went rapidly towards the masked door, and had just time to let the tapestry drop behind her, when Judas entered, preceded by the servant.

"Monsieur Guinaud!"

The servant retired, and Judas in his dark dress, with a crafty look on his bloodless face, stood looking at Mr. Marson.

"Will you be seated, sir?" said the latter gentleman, indicating a chair.

"Wis pleasure, monsieur," said Judas, bowing. "Speak you de français, monsieur?"

"Oui."

"Très bien," replied Guinaud, with a satisfied smile; "let us speak my tongue, monsieur, if you please! I am not at home in your English!"

He sat down with a self-satisfied smile, drew his gloves off his long, lean hands, and having thrown open his overcoat, rubbed his hands together slowly, as he looked at Marson with his most guileless expression.

"Eh! my faith, but it is cold in this England of yours," he said, passing his hand over his smooth red hair. "I am a child of the South, me, and find these skies of rain not pleasant, after my beautiful Provence."

"What do you want to see me about?" asked Marson, sharply, taking an instinctive dislike to the sleek, treacherous manner of Judas. "I cannot spare you much time, so please be quick."

Judas shrugged his shoulders, smiled blandly, and came to the point by slow degrees.

"I am the friend of the late Sebastian Melstane, monsieur."

"I have heard that!"

"Alas! he is dead!"

"I have heard that, also!"

"Eh! you know much, monsieur. Do you also know that he was murdered?"

"Good heavens! No!"

Monsieur Guinaud lifted his eyes to heaven with a sad smile.

"But yes, certainly, monsieur. He died from a pill of morphia placed in his box of pills of tonic, which he had from the shop of Monsieur Vosk."

"Who put the pill in the box?"

"Eh! monsieur, do you not know?"

"Of course I don't."

Judas narrowed his eyes down to their dangerous expression, and shrugged his shoulders once more, but said nothing.

"And what has Melstane's death to do with me?" asked Marson, coldly.

"Monsieur, he loved your child."

"I am aware of that. A piece of infernal impertinence."

"Then you are glad of his death?"

182

"I am neither glad nor sorry, Monsieur Guinaud. I don't know why you have done me the honour to seek this interview. If you will state your reason, I will be pleased."

The Frenchman leaned back in his chair, placed the tips of his long fingers together, and smiled sweetly.

"Monsieur Mar-rson, my friend that loved your beautiful child is dead. I am full of regrets for him, but for myself I have the pleasure."

"And why?"

"Can you not guess the secret of my heart? I love your angel."

"You!"

Marson had sprung to his feet and was now looking angrily at the Frenchman, who, without moving his position, still smiled blandly.

"Even I, Jules Guinaud."

The other looked at him in a contemptuous fashion; then, without a word, walked across to the fireplace and put out his hand to touch the ivory knob of the electric bell.

"One moment, monsieur," said Judas, raising his voice slightly; "what do you intend to do?"

"Have you turned out of my house."

He pressed the knob, and remained standing by the fireplace in disdainful silence; but Judas, laughing softly, leaned back in his chair.

"Eh, truly? I think not. You won't do that when you hear

what I've got to say."

The servant appeared at the door.

"When you see, monsieur, what I can show you."

"Marks, show this gentleman out."

Judas took no notice of the order, but walked across the room with the feline grace of a tiger and whispered something in Marson's ear. The old man started, turned deadly white, and with an effort spoke again to the servant.

"You can go at present, Marks. I will ring if I want you."

The servant retired and Guinaud returned to his seat, leaving Marson still standing by the fireplace. Now, however, he looked faint and ill, clinging to the mantelpiece for support. At length with an effort he pulled himself together, and staggered rather than walked to his seat.

"What are your proofs?" he asked Guinaud, in a harsh whisper.

Monsieur Judas, with the same stereotyped smile on his face, took some papers out of his breast coat-pocket, and, still retaining his hold of them, spread them out before Marson.

A single look was sufficient.

"My God!" cried Marson, with sudden terror; "I—I—my God!"

* * * * *

Judith, anxious to know the reason of Guinaud's visit, had rapidly changed her dress, and was about to go down again to the study when Florry's nurse called her in to look at the invalid. The girl was in one of those terrible paroxysms of excitement, common to delirium, when sick people possess unnatural strength, and Judith had to aid the nurse to hold her down. This took some time, and when at length Florry was lying comparatively quiet, Judith found that she had lost more than half an hour.

At once she went downstairs again and entered the adjacent room, intending to make her appearance by the curtained door. As she stood with her hand on the lock, the door being slightly ajar, she heard Guinaud's voice raised in triumph.

"Of course, monsieur, you will now permit me to be a suitor for the hand of Mees Mar-rson?"

Hardly believing her ears, Judith listened intently for Marson's reply, but when it came it was so low that she could not hear it, and she only gathered its purport from the next observation of the Frenchman.

"You must! Remember, I know all."

"I cannot! I cannot! Besides, my daughter is ill—seriously ill."

"Ah, bah! she will get well, the dear angel."

"But she is to marry Mr. Spolger."

"Quite a mistake, monsieur. She is to marry me! Eh, what do you say?"

"No."

Guinaud and Marson both turned round, to see Judith standing beside them with a look of anger on her face.

"I say, no," she reiterated.

"Eh, mademoiselle, but you are not the father," said Judas, with a sneer.

"You marry Miss Marson," cried Judith, angrily; "you! How dare you, sir, come to the house of an English gentleman and make such a request? You—you—thief!"

"Thief, mademoiselle!" said the Frenchman, smiling.

"Yes! I know that you have stolen some letters from that packet addressed to me."

"Eh, but it is true, mademoiselle. I have just been showing them to Monsieur Mar-rson, and he is so delighted, this dear monsieur, that he says to me: 'Take now the charming angel, Jules; she is for you.'"

"I don't believe it! I don't believe it!" cried Judith, turning towards the old man. "Mr. Marson, you will never consent to give your daughter to this low spy!"

"Eh, mademoiselle, you are not polite."

"Speak to this man, Mr. Marson; tell him you refuse to do his bidding."

The old man raised his hands helplessly and sighed.

"I cannot, Judith; I cannot."

"You will give Florry to this man for his wife!"

"I must."

"You see, mademoiselle—"

"Be silent, monsieur," she said, haughtily; "I do not speak to you. Francis Marson, your daughter was left to my charge by your dead wife, and I say she shall not marry this man."

"Judith! Judith! I have seen—I have seen the papers."

"Ah!" said Judith, with a long-drawn breath, "you have seen the papers."

"But yes, certainly," observed Judas, with a sneer. "And having seen them, monsieur is prepared to give me his child. Is it not so?"

Marson nodded his head mechanically, but Judith, standing beside him, turned suddenly on the smiling Frenchman with such vehemence, that he recoiled from her fury.

"You have threatened an old man," she hissed, angrily. "You have learned a secret by chance, and you use it for your own base ends. But it shall not be; I say it shall not be."

"And I say it shall be," said Judas, slipping off his smiling mask. "Listen to me, mademoiselle. I come to you now with peace; let me go without my wishes being gratified, and I return with war. Eh! I mock myself of your anger. Bah! I care not for your wrath; not I! See you here, Miss Var-rlins. In the one hand I hold, silence; in the other, ruin and exposure. Choose which you will. The world does not know how my friend Melstane came by his end. I speak, and all is told!"

Judith had fallen on her knees, and was hiding her white face against the chair on which sat Francis Marson; and he, worn, anguished, and terror-stricken, was looking in horror on the gibing enemy of them both.

"You kneel now—you kneel to me," cried Judas, mockingly, "to me—the spy, the thief! Eh, but I remember all. There is a guillotine in your land; but yes, I know it is so. One word from me and them—oh, you know it well, I see, you gentle English lady. I could speak on and ruin all, but I am a man of honour. I wish to be kind, and I say to this dear monsieur what will be my desire. Now I go for a time—for a day. When I come back it is for you to say what you will. Good night, my friends. Guinaud is no fool. He holds the cards and he wins the game! chut!"

He walked out of the room with a mocking laugh, leaving Judith crouched in abject terror by the side of the old man, who sat as if turned to stone.

Chapter 14

Who is Guilty?

Dr. Japix was a bachelor, and therefore, by all the laws of domesticity, should have been badly served as far as regards home comforts; but then Dr. Japix had a good housekeeper so was served excellently well in every respect. For instance, his dinners were famous for the quality of the food and wines, as Fanks and his friend Axton found by practical experience when they dined with their unwedded host. He gave them a capital meal, undeniable wine, and as all three men were good conversationalists, they had a very delightful dinner. Afterwards, they went to the Doctor's study, a particularly comfortable room, and smoked wonderfully good cigars over first-rate coffee.

The study was a private snuggery especially affected by the Doctor, who had in it all his books, a few comfortable chairs, an enticing-looking writing-table, some good etchings by eminent artists, and plenty of warm red draperies to keep out the cold winds so general in Ironfields. On this night there was a blazing fire in the polished grate, and around it sat Japix and his two guests, enjoying the soothing weed and talking about the Jarlchester case. Luckily, Japix was perfectly free on this special night, and unless some unexpected call should be made on him, was permitted by those hard laws which regulate the lives of medical men to enjoy his smoke and talk to his friends as he pleased. All three had plenty to say, and as the night wore on towards the small hours, they gradually began to talk of Melstane's murder, a topic to which everything had been tending for a considerable time. It is true that they had referred to it in a desultory fashion, but it was not until ten o'clock that they settled down to a steady analysis of the case.

"Most extraordinary," said Japix, in his subdued roar; "reflects great credit on you, Fanks, for the way in which you have found it out."

"I've not got to the end of my journey yet," replied Octavius, grimly, "so I won't holloa till I'm out of the wood."

"You're out of the Jarlchester wood, at all events."

"Yes, only to plunge into the deeper recesses of the Ironfields wood."

"Well," said Axton, reflectively, "you've proved conclusively that I did not commit the crime."

"You!" shouted Japix, in amazement.

"Yes, I!" replied Roger, serenely. "Just fancy, Doctor, you are sitting with a suspected murderer."

"Not now," remonstrated Fanks, good-humouredly; "if I did suspect you for a moment, you soon cleared yourself in my eyes. But you must admit things looked black against you."

"So black," assented Axton, quickly, "that had the detective been any other than yourself, I should now be in prison awaiting my trial on a charge of attempted murder."

"Possibly," answered Fanks, lighting a fresh cigar; "not only that but even probably. However, you have proved your innocence, and Spolger has proved his."

"Did you suspect him also?" asked the Doctor, chuckling. "I thought as much from your questions to-day, Monsieur Fouché."

"Well, he had the fatal pill-box in his possession; he uses morphia for his Soothers; he hated Melstane, so altogether —"

"There was a very nice little case against him," finished Japix, with a gigantic laugh. "Oh, I know your profession Monsieur Lecoq; I have read Gaboriau's romances."

"I'm afraid we're not so infallible as the great Lecoq."

"Pooh! why not? I dare say he's modelled on Vidocq. At all events, you've now got an enigma which would delight Monsieur Gaboriau."

"Real life is more difficult than fiction."

"There you are wrong. Fiction is a reflection of real life—a holding of the mirror up to Nature. Eh—author?"

"Shakespeare," said Octavius, promptly, "and quoted wrongly."

"Never mind; the spirit if not the form is there."

"We've strayed from the subject," observed Axton, smiling, "regarding this case. Since Spolger and myself are innocent, who is guilty?"

"Ask something easier."

"Do you know, my good Vidocq," remarked Japix, contemplating his large feet, "that I wonder you have not turned your attention to Monsieur Judas."

"I have done so," said Octavius, quietly; "but I can bring nothing home to him. He's very clever."

"A scoundrel's virtue."

"Yes, and a scoundrel's safety."

"Didn't you tell me the other day that you thought Judas held all the threads of the case in his hand?" said Roger, turning to Fanks.

"I fancy I said something like that," replied Octavius, slowly; "but, if I mistake not, you had suspicions of Judas yourself."

"Had," said Roger, emphatically; "no, have! I have suspicions of Judas, and I'm pretty sure—"

"That he committed the murder," finished the Doctor.

"Oh, I'm not prepared to go that far," said Fanks, quickly;

"but as regards Monsieur Guinaud, I'll tell you one thing. It's the custom, I understand, for the master to check the assistant with regard to the number of pills in a box."

"Yes; that is the usual custom."

"Well, I understood from Judas that such was the case with Melstane's tonic pills. Having my suspicions, however, I went and saw Wosk myself."

"And what did he say?"

"That he counted the pills in the box and then handed it back to Judas—open."

"Oh," said Axton, suddenly, "then you think it was Judas put the two extra pills in the box?"

"He might have done so."

"But what would be his motive in getting rid of Melstane?"

"Ah, there's no difficulty in answering that," replied Fanks, quickly. "It appears Judas loves Miss Marson to distraction; Melstane stood in his way, so he might have got rid of him by the pill method."

"Granted," said Japix, eagerly; "but even if he did remove Melstane by that morphia method, he would be no nearer the object of his love than before. A chemist's assistant is not a fitting match for the heiress of Francis Marson."

"True, true!"

"Besides," said Axton, taking up the defence, "why should Judas take the trouble to kill Melstane at Jarlchester when he could have done so at Ironfields?"

"Oh, that's merely a question of safety," replied Octavius, thoughtfully. "If Melstane had died here, awkward questions might have been asked, which would have been difficult for Guinaud to answer; but at Jarlchester the man dies, and there is nothing to connect Judas or any one else with the death. That pill idea is a devilish ingenious one."

"Quite worthy of a Frenchman!"

"Pooh! the virtuous English can easily hold their own in that respect; for every extraordinary case in Paris I can find you an equivalent in London."

"By the way," cried Japix, suddenly deserting the line of conversation in favour of a new one, "I went to see Miss Marson to-day; she's very ill, you know."

"My fault," said Roger, regretfully, "blurting out the fact of Melstane's death."

"Well, go on," said Fanks, impatiently; "what were you going to say, Japix?"

"That I visited Miss Marson to-day."

"You've said that. What else?"

"And I saw her father, who told me a most extraordinary thing."

"Wait a bit," said the detective, with great excitement. "I'll bet you a fiver that I can tell you what he told you."

"The deuce you can!" replied Japix, in astonishment. "Well, I'll take the bet. Marson said?"

"That Judas had written him asking him for an interview."

"Right! How the—no, I won't swear. But how, by all that's sacred, did you find that out?"

"And Judas also said it was about some documents."

"Right again! I believe you are a magician, Fanks."

"Not at all—inductive reasoning."

"I wish you'd stop talking riddles," broke in Roger, irritably, "and tell us what the deuce you mean."

"It won't be very pleasant—to your ears."

"Go on. I know what you're going to say," said Roger, excitedly, "but don't mind me. I'm going to know the truth about this business."

Japix looked at his two guests with astonishment depicted on his broad, good-humoured face, but judged it best to say nothing until Octavius explained matters, which he did speedily.

"My dear Japix," he said, quietly, "there was a packet of letters which Roger obtained from Melstane at Jarlchester and forwarded to Miss Varlins, addressed to her by her first name."

"Miss Judith!"

"Precisely! Well, that stupid old postmistress muddled up the name with that of Judas, and sent the packet to him. We met Miss Varlins, and went together to get the packet from Guinaud. I asked her to let me see the packet. She refused at first, but ultimately consented on condition that I let her look over the letters first. I agreed to that, she did so, and I found nothing."

"Well, well!" said Japix, quickly, "I don't see anything strange in that."

"Don't you? I do! If there had been nothing particular in that packet, Miss Varlins would not have objected to my seeing it. So my belief is that Judas abstracted the letters he did not want me to see, and has gone to Marson to show them to him."

"Well!"

"Well!" repeated Fanks, angrily, "don't you see? Those letters, stolen by Judas, bear indirectly on the death of Melstane."

"If that is the case, why should Judas show them to Marson?"

Fanks fidgeted uneasily in his chair, looked at the floor, the ceiling, the Doctor, everywhere but at Roger.

"I really can't tell," he said at length, very lamely.

"Yes, you can," shouted Roger, rising quickly; "you suspect —"

"I have said no name," replied Fanks, very pale, rising in his turn.

"No, but I will!"

"Roger!"

"I will tell you, and I declare it's a lie—a lie!"

"Good heavens!" cried Japix, rising, "what does this mean?"

He looked at both men for an answer, and obtained it from Roger:

"It means that my old schoolfellow suspects the woman I love of a crime."

"Judith Varlins!"

"Yes; Judith Varlins!"

Japix looked at Fanks to see if he would repeat the accusation, but the detective said nothing.

"My dear Axton, you're dreaming," he said, soothingly. "I'd as soon think of suspecting myself."

Roger seized the large hand of the Doctor and shook it heartily.

"Thank Heaven there is some one believes her innocent," he said, with a half sob.

"Tut, tut!" answered the Doctor, quietly, "sit down, my dear boy, sit down. There must be some explanation of this."

"If Roger would not be so impetuous," said Fanks, who had resumed his seat, "I would like to tell him something."

Roger looked at his friend with a gleam of hope in his eye, and sat down in sullen silence.

"You yourself say I suspect Miss Varlins," explained Fanks, with faint hesitation, "simply because I said Judas had taken certain documents to Marson. How do you know that I may not suspect some one else?"

"Whom?"

"Miss Varlins," observed Fanks, leisurely, "may, for all we know, be acting a very noble part, and may be trying to screen another person—for instance, Mr. Francis Marson."

"What?" shouted Japix and Roger in one breath.

"I'm not certain—by no means certain; but I have my suspicions."

"Of Marson?" said Japix, scornfully; "pooh! nonsense! There isn't a more respected man in Ironfields."

"It's generally your respected persons who fancy they can sin with impunity, and not be found out on account of that very respectability. May I ask you a few questions, Japix?"

"By all means."

"Why did Marson want his pretty daughter to marry that ugly wreck of a Spolger?"

Japix hesitated a moment before answering.

"I know nothing for a fact," he said at length, with great reluctance, "but common rumour—"

"Common rumour by all means. There's no smoke without fire."

"A detestable proverb," said Japix, frowning. "Well, rumour says that Marson will smash if money is not put into his business, and that Florry Marson was to be the price of Spolger finding for Marson & Son the requisite money."

"I think that's the most powerful reason for the crime we've had yet."

Neither of his listeners answered this remark, as they seemed instinctively to feel that the fatal net was closing round Marson through the relentless logic of the detective.

"In the case of Axton," resumed Fanks, coolly, "the motive

for the crime appeared to be love. In the case of Spolger, love. In the case of Judas, love. All very well, but hardly a strong enough motive to make a man put a rope round his neck. In this case of Marson, however, what do we find? Bankruptcy, loss of position, loss of money, loss of name, in fact, loss of everything that a man holds most dear. A strong motive, I think."

"I can't stand this," cried Roger, jumping up quickly; "confound it, Fanks, you'd argue the man guilty without a chance of defence. You tell us the motive for the crime, certainly; but how did Marson do it? When did he have the pill-box? Where could he obtain the morphia?"

"Judas knows."

"Judas!"

"Yes. I believe Judas is an accomplice of Marson, and between the two of them they killed Melstane in that remarkably ingenious manner."

"I can't believe it," said Japix, as his two visitors arose to take their leave.

"Probably not," replied Fanks, calmly; "but I'll give you plenty of proof shortly."

"Why, what do you intend to do?"

"I'm going to see Monsieur Judas."

"You'll find him a match for you," said the Doctor, grimly, as he accompanied his guests to the door.

"Then I'll see Marson."

"Humph! two stools, you'll fall to the ground."

"I'll take my chance of that," said Fanks, cheerfully, as he stepped out into the darkness with Roger. "Good night, Japix. I'll be able to give you the key to the Jarlchester Mystery next week."

Extracts From a Detectives Note-Book

". . . Just returned from an evening with Japix . . . We (R., J., and myself) had a long conversation about the case . . . This conversation has left me in a state of great perplexity . . . I told Japix I would give him the key to the mystery next week, but I spoke more boldly than I have reason to . . . It is true I am narrowing down the circle . . . I suspect two people, with a possible third . . . Marson, Judith Varlins, and Judas . . . It's a very humiliating fact to confess this indecision even to myself . . . But, detectives are not infallible save in novels . . . I am perplexed . . . I have suspected Axton wrongfully . . . I have suspected Spolger wrongfully, and now . . . Let me make a note of the motives of each of the three people I suspect now . . .

". . . Marson! He is on the verge of bankruptcy . . . only one person can save him, viz. Jackson Spolger . . . He, however, declines to help him unless he marries Florry Marson . . . She won't marry Spolger because of her love for Melstane . . . A strong motive here for Marson to get rid of Melstane . . .

". . . Miss Varlins . . . Her motive for getting rid of Melstane, I think, is a mixture of love and jealousy . . . Both strong motives, with a woman . . .

". . . Judas! He loves Miss Marson also, and with his loose

morality would have no hesitation in putting Melstane out of the way. He wants Florry Marson, he wants her money . . . Melstane stands in the way of his obtaining both . . . in such a case Judas is just the man — from my reading of his character — to commit a crime . . . Again, his employment as a chemist offers him peculiar advantages for obtaining morphia . . . It would be difficult for either Marson or Miss Varlins to obtain morphia in a large quantity, but Judas could easily get it in the ordinary course of his business . . . I am going to see Judas, and from a second conversation may perhaps learn something useful . . . He is crafty . . . still he may betray himself . . . at all events, it is worth while trying.

"*Mem.* — To see Judas to-morrow night."

Chapter 15

Monsieur Judas at Bay

Monsieur Jules Guinaud was not quite satisfied in his own mind with regard to the result of his interview of the previous night. It was true that by using the documents he had stolen from Melstane's packet he had succeeded in obtaining Marson's consent to his marriage with Florry, but it was also true that he had found an unexpected obstacle to his plans in the person of Judith Varlins. He was cynical in his estimate of the female sex, regarding them as beings quite inferior to the male, but at the same time he was too clever a man to underestimate the result of a quick-witted woman opposing herself to his will. Florry was a mere cypher, whom he loved in a sensual fashion for her beauty, and in a worldly fashion for her money, but Judith was quite a different stamp of woman to this negative type of inane loveliness. She had a masculine brain, she had a strong will, she had a fearless nature, and Guinaud dreaded the upshot of any interference on her part.

A genius, this man—a genius in a wicked way, with wonderful capabilities of arranging his plans, and brushing aside any obstacle that might interfere with their fulfilment, In this case Judith interfered, so Judas, taking a rapid survey of the situation, saw a means by which he could silence her effectively, and determined to do so without delay. He wished to marry Florry Marson; he wished to enjoy the income, the position, and the benefits derived from being a son-in-law of Marson, and was consequently determined to let nothing stand in the way of the realisation of his hopes. Judas was not a brave man, but he was wonderfully crafty, and the fox, as a rule, gains his ends where the lion fails; so the Frenchman determined to go up to the Hall on the night following his first interview, see Judith, and let her know at once what to expect if she meddled with his arrangements.

This was all very nicely arranged, and if Monsieur Guinaud had been undisturbed, he would no doubt have succeeded in his wicked little plans; but Fate, not approving of this usurpation of her role as arbitrator of human lives, interfered, and Octavius Fanks was the instrument she used to defeat all the Frenchman's schemes.

In playing with Fate, that goddess has a nasty habit of forcing her opponent's hand before he desires to show it, and this is what she did now, to the great discomfiture of Monsieur Judas.

It was about eight o'clock on the night following that momentous interview at the Hall, and all Mrs. Binter's boarders had left the jail on the ticket of-leave system except Judas, who sat in the drawing-room cell arranging everything in his crafty brain before setting out on his errand to Miss Varlins. The head-jailer had several times entered the room and intimated that he had better run out for a breath of fresh air; but Judas, saying he would go later on, kept his seat by the diminutive fire, and declined to obey Mrs. Binter, much to that good lady's disgust.

"Why, drat the man," she said, in her stony fashion, to one of the under-warders, "what does he mean by wastin' coals an' ile? Why don't he walk his dinner off by usin' his legs instead of robbin' me of my profits by takin' it out of his thirty shillin's weekly?"

The under-warder suggested respectfully that Monsieur Judas might be expecting a friend that night, as on a previous occasion, to which the jailer made prompt reply:

"Oh, I dare say! That friend he had here was a furriner. I heard 'em talking their French gabble. It's more like a turkey gobblin' than a man talkin'. Why don't these furriners learn English? There's the front-door bell! P'r'aps it's that friend again. I'll go myself."

And go herself she did, to find Mr. Fanks waiting on the doorstep; and thinking he was expected by Judas, seeing that gentleman had waited in, took him in charge, and formally conducted him to the drawing-room cell.

"A gentleman for you, munseer," she said, glaring at her lodger, who had arisen to his feet in some surprise, "an' please don't use too many coals, sir. For coals is coals, however much you may think 'em waste-paper."

Having thus relieved her feelings, Mrs. Binter retired to the basement, where she amused herself with badgering Mr. Binter, and Fanks was left alone with the chemist's assistant.

"You wish to see me, monsieur?" asked Judas, in French, narrowing his eyes to their most catlike expression.

"Yes," replied Fanks, sitting down. "I wish to ask you a few questions."

"I cannot give you long, Monsieur Fanks," said the Frenchman, unwillingly, "I have an engagement for this night!"

"Oh, indeed. With Mr. Marson, or Miss Varlins?" This was carrying the war into the enemy's camp with a vengeance, and for a moment Judas was so nonplussed, that he did not know what to say.

"Monsieur is pleased to be amusing," he said, at length, with an ugly smile. "Monsieur does me the honour to make my business his own."

"I'm glad you see my intentions so clearly, Monsieur Guinaud."

They were painfully polite to one another, these two men, but this mutual politeness was of a dangerous kind foreboding a storm. Like two skilful fencers, they watched one another warily, each ready to take advantage of the first opportunity to break down the guard of the other. It was difficult to say who would win, for they were equally clever, equally watchful, equally merciless, and neither of them underestimated the acuteness of his adversary. A duel of brains, both men on guard, and Fanks made the first attack!

"Are you aware, Monsieur Guinaud, that you stand in a

very dangerous position?"

"My faith, no! Not at all."

"Then it is as well you should know at once. I am a detective, as you know, and am investigating this affair of your late friend. I suspect some one of the murder."

"Very well. Monsieur Axton?"

"No."

"The dear Spolgers?"

"No."

Judas shrugged his shoulders!

"My faith! I know not, then, the man you suspect."

"Yes, you do. I suspect Monsieur Jules Guinaud."

The Frenchman was by no means startled, but laughed jeeringly.

"Eh, monsieur! Que diable faites-vous dans cette galère?"

"You need not jest. I am in earnest!"

"Truly! Will monsieur speak plainly?"

"Certainly! You say you were a friend of Melstane's. That is a lie. You hated him because he was your successful rival with Miss Marson. You wished him dead, so that you would be free to make your suit to the young lady. The box of tonic pills left your hands for those of Melstane."

"Pardon! It went first into the hands of Monsieur Vosk."

204

"Don't trouble to tell lies, Guinaud. I have asked Wosk, and he says he counted the pills, and then gave you the box again—open."

"It's a lie!"

"Reserve your defence, if you please. When you got that box, you put in those two morphia pills, and Melstane left Ironfields carrying his death in his pocket."

"You have the invention, monsieur, I see."

"In this scheme for Melstane's death you were prompted by your accomplice, Francis Marson."

"Eh! It's an excellent play, without doubt."

"You stole some compromising letters of Marson's from that packet of Melstane's, and took them up to him last night."

"You are wisdom itself, monsieur."

"Those letters form your hold over Marson, and you offered to destroy them on condition that he let you marry Miss Marson."

"A miracle of logic! Eh, I believe well."

"It is my firm conviction," said Fanks, losing his temper at the gibing tones of the Frenchman, "that what I have stated is the truth, and that you and Marson are responsible for the death of Melstane in the way I have described."

"Monsieur is not afraid of the law of libel, evidently."

"No; there are no witnesses present."

"Ah, you scheme well?"

"Pshaw! What answer can you make to my statement?"

Monsieur Judas smiled blandly, shrugged his shoulders, and spread out his lean hands with a deprecating gesture.

"Me! Alas! I can say nothing but that you have as strong a case against me as you had against your dear friend, Monsieur Roger."

Fanks reddened angrily. He was aware that he had blundered two or three times during the case, but still it was not pleasant to be taunted thus by a smiling adversary who indulged in fine irony.

"You led me to believe Axton was guilty," he said, meekly.

"I? Eh, it is a mistake. I but told what I knew. It is not my fault if the affair reflects upon Monsieur Roger."

"Do you know I can arrest you on suspicion of murder?"

"Truly! Then do so. I am ready."

Fanks bit his nails in impotent wrath, feeling himself quite helpless to deal with this man. He could not arrest him because he had not sufficient evidence to warrant him doing so. He could not force him to speak, as he had no means of commanding him. Altogether he was completely at the mercy of Judas in every way. Judas saw this and chuckled.

"Can I tell monsieur anything else?"

"Confound you, sir, you've told me nothing."

"Eh, it is because I do know nothing."

"That is a lie, Guinaud. I believe you know all about this case."

"Monsieur does me too much honour."

It was very provoking, certainly, and Fanks, seeing the uselessness of prolonging the discussion, was about to retire when a sudden thought entered his head.

"At all events Monsieur Guinaud," he said, deliberately, "cool as you are now, you may not be quite so composed before a judge."

"Ah! you will arrest me for the murder. Well, I wait, monsieur, for your pleasure. Bah! I am no child to be frightened by big drums."

"I won't arrest you for the murder, but I will for stealing those letters."

Judas winced at this. He was not very well acquainted with English law, and although he knew Fanks would not dare to arrest him on a charge of murder on the present evidence, yet he was by no means certain regarding the business of the letters. He thought a moment.

"You will arrest me for stealing what you do not know that I did steal?"

"What I know or what I don't know doesn't matter. I'll arrest you as soon as I can obtain a warrant. Once you are in the clutches of the English law, and you won't get out of them till you tell all you know about this case."

Octavius was simply playing a game of bluff with Judas trusting to the Frenchman's ignorance of English law to win him the game. He was right in this case, as Guinaud did not know how far the arm of Justice could stretch in England, and thought he might be arrested for the theft of the letters. If so, it would be fatal to his schemes, as he desired to avoid publicity in every way, and arrest at present meant the tumbling down of his carefully built house of cards. Having thus taken a rapid survey of the position, he made up his mind to save himself by the sacrifice of some one else, and he fixed upon Judith, who had tried to thwart him, as the victim. With this idea he politely desired Fanks to be seated again—a request which that gentleman obeyed with a feeling of great relief, as he had played his last card in a desperate game, and was grateful to find that it had turned up trumps.

The detective therefore seated himself once more, but Judas, foreseeing a fine opportunity of exercising his oratorical talents, remained standing, and waved his hand in a loftily theatrical manner.

"Monsieur," he said, with apparent grief, "you see before you a man of honour. It is all that I have, this honour of my forefathers, and I would not sell it, no! not for the wealth of the Monte Cristo of our dear Dumas. But in this case it is one of justice. If I am silent I am suspected of a terrible crime; my name is in the dust. Can I let it lie there? But no, it is impossible; so to myself I say, 'You must forget your honour for once, and speak the name of that woman.'"

"Woman!"

"Eh! monsieur, you are astonished. It is not strange! Listen to me! I will tell you what I know of my dear friend's death."

"But you're not going to tell me a woman killed him?" Guinaud placed his left hand inside his waistcoat, and waved the right, solemnly.

"Monsieur! There are terrible things in this world. The heart of man is not good, but the heart of woman—ah! who can

208

explore its depths? Not even our Balzac, of all the most profound—"

"Hang your preaching, get on with your story."

Monsieur Judas smiled, dropped his pompous manner, and told his little tale in a highly dramatic fashion.

"I speak then, monsieur, straight. It's a drama of the Porte St. Martin. In this way. On the night before my dear friend goes to Jarlcesterre he is in this room; with him, myself. We talk, we laugh, we weep adieu! At once there is a tap at the window there—the window that opens like a door on to the beautiful grass. We turn; I see the dress, the hood, the figure of a woman, but not the face. My friend Sebastian to me speaks: 'Go, my good friend, I have to speak with a charming angel. You are a man of honour. Disturb not our rendezvous.' What would you? I go, and my friend Sebastian locks the door. At this I am angry. He trusts me not, so I say: 'Very well, you think I am a spy. So be it, I will listen.' Conceive to yourself, monsieur, how I was judged. In anger, I went outside to that window. It is open but a little, and I hear all—all! Sebastian to the woman speaks. They talk, and talk, and fight, and rage! Oh! it was terrible. She asks of him something, and he says, 'Yes, it is for you.' Then he goes out of this room by that door. She is left alone, this charming woman. She goes to the table, here; on it there is a box of pills—my friend's box of pills. She opens the box. My eye beholds her drop into it something, I know not what. Again she closes the box, and waits. I see my dear Melstane return. They talk, they kiss, they part. From the window I fly, and when I come into this room by the door, the woman is gone, Sebastian is gone, and the window is closed but not locked. I go to it, I open it, and on the grass there I see a handkerchief; it is now mine, and on it is the name of the woman that came—the woman that put the pills in the box—the woman that killed my friend."

"And the name—the name!" cried Fanks, in a state of great excitement, springing to his feet; "tell me her name."

Rapid as thought Guinaud produced a white handkerchief from his breast-pocket and flung it to Fanks.

The detective seized it, and looked at the name in the corner.

"Judith!"

Extracts From a Detective's Note-Book

". . . I have seen Judas, and he made a strange confession . . . He actually saw the person who committed the crime put the pills into the box . . . The name was hardly a surprise to me . . . I thought Miss Varlins was guilty, but hardly thought my suspicions would be confirmed so soon . . . Poor Roger, it will be a terrible blow to him to learn that the woman he loves is guilty of such a terrible crime . . . I don't believe she ever loved Roger . . . all her passions were centred on Melstane . . . He must have been a wonderfully fascinating scamp . . . I don't know why I should pity Judith Varlins . . . She has treated Roger shamefully . . . She has treated Florry Marson shamefully . . . for she pretended to love the one and killed the lover of the other . . . Her handkerchief has betrayed her . . . She will be a very clever woman if she can get out of that . . . The evidence of the handkerchief . . . the evidence of Judas are both dead against her . . .

"*Mem.*—To write to Marson asking for an interview.

". . . I will take up Judas and Roger with me, so as to convict

210

her of the crime . . . It will be a terrible ordeal for the poor boy, but anything is better than that he should marry a murderess . . . This was the reason she refused to let me see the letters . . . some of her own were there, betraying her guilty passion . . . She has been playing a double game all through, but now she is brought to book at last . . . She must be a woman of iron nerve . . . Her adopted sister is lying dangerously ill from the consequences of Judith's crime . . . from the sudden intelligence that the man she loved is dead, and yet Judith can still wear her mask and play the part of a sick-nurse . . . She must be a perfect fiend . . . Lucrezia Borgia *fin de siècle* . . . I expect to have a terrible scene to-morrow night . . . Poor Roger! . . .

"Judas is an incarnate devil . . . I wish he was the guilty one instead of Judith Varlins . . . Nothing would give me greater pleasure than to put the irons on him."

Chapter 16

The Man Who Loved Her

Have you ever been in the tropics? If so, you must know how cruel the sun can be to the unhappy Europeans grilling under its ardent rays. It does not invigorate, nor tan the skin overmuch, nor make one think life is a good thing; but it enervates the system, it relaxes the muscles, it dulls the brain, until the body is nothing but a worn-out shell, that moves, and rests, and lies down, and stands up in a mechanical fashion, like an automaton. It was like this that Judith felt after the terrible interview with Guinaud, and she went the round of her daily duties in a dull, listless manner, that showed how greatly her vital force had been exhausted by the ordeal she had undergone. With constant attendance on the invalid, and anxious thoughts about the position of affairs with regard to the Frenchman, she was worn out mentally and physically.

At present it was difficult to come to any decision relative to Florry's illness as the crisis had not yet come, and youth, health, and love of life were all fighting desperately against the shadow of death. The shock sustained by Florry on hearing of the untimely end of her lover had quite unsettled her brain, and the balance was trembling between health and sickness, between sanity and insanity, between life and death. She needed constant watching, for at times, in the most unexpected manner, she would spring from her bed and try to leave the room, bound on some fantastic journey created by the excited state of her brain. At other times she lay languid and exhausted, with dim, unseeing eyes, raving madly about her lover and the unforeseen calamity of his death. Afraid to trust this fragile life to the care of a hired nurse, Judith herself sat by the bedside, and ministered to the wants of the sick girl, holding the cool drink to the fevered lips, bathing the feverish brow, and arranging with loving hand the disordered bed-clothes.

It was bad enough in the day to sit in the twilight of the sick-room listening to the aimless chatter that came from the white lips, but it was worse at night. The sombre shadows that hung over all, the faint glimmer of the shaded lamp, the uncanny stillness of the house, and nothing awake but the sick girl with her pathetic pleadings, her causeless laughter, and the incessant stream of disconnected wanderings. No wonder Judith was quite worn out with constant watching; much, however, as she needed rest, she never surrendered her weary post by the bed, but sat, watchful and tender, during the long hours, only calling in the nurse when the paroxysms seized the invalid. All through the endless night succeeding the interview she had sat like a stone image in the sick-room, going over in her own tortured mind all that Guinaud had said. The morning broke dull and gray, and the nurse insisted upon her resting for a time. Rest! there was no such luxury for her; for even when lying down, her weary brain went mechanically over the old ground, imagining a thousand terrors, and agonising itself with a thousand pangs.

At last she slept for a time, but it was no refreshing slumber such as would bring relief. No! nothing but dreams, strange, horrible dreams, in all of which Judas, cruel and merciless, was the central figure; so in despair of gaining quiet in any way, she arose in the afternoon, and returned to her post by the side of Florry.

At four o'clock a card was brought to her bearing the name of Roger Axton, and a few lines scribbled thereon asking her to see him at once. With a start of terror, she wondered whether Judas had been to Axton, and revealed anything; but remembering that silence was as necessary to Judas as to herself, she dismissed this fear as idle, and having called in the nurse, descended to the drawing-room.

Roger was there, pacing restlessly to and fro like a caged lion, but when she entered he stopped at once, and looked at her fixedly as she came towards him in her sweeping black dress. Worn and haggard both of them, anxious and apprehensive both of them, they looked like two criminals meeting for the first time after the commission of a secret crime.

213

On seeing Roger's altered face, Judith also paused and gazed at him with a terrified look in her dilated eyes. They stood silently looking at one another for a single moment, but in that moment the agony of a lifetime was concentrated.

At last Roger spoke in a low, smothered tone, as if the words issued from his white lips against his will.

"No! no! I cannot believe it."

This speech broke the strange spell that held Judith motionless, and stealing forward she touched him lightly on the shoulder as he sank into a chair, covering his wild face with his hands.

"Roger!"

No answer. Only the short quick breath of the man and the soft rustle of the woman's dress.

"Roger, what is the matter?"

He looked up suddenly, hollow-eyed and shrinking, with a wild, questioning look on his worn face.

"I—I—have been told something."

"By—by that Frenchman?"

"Yes!"

"My God!" she muttered to herself, falling nerveless into a chair, "what has he told him?"

"He has told me all!"

"All?"

"He has told not only me but Fanks!"

214

"The detective?"

"Yes."

She hid her face in her hands with a startled cry, at which he sprang quickly from his chair and flung himself on his knees beside her.

"Oh, my love—my love!" he cried, entreatingly, "you are innocent; you are innocent. I know you are!"

"I innocent?"

She was looking down at him with an expression of amazement on her face, the beauty of which was marred by tears, by weariness, and by anxious thought.

"Yes! I'll swear you did not kill him!"

"Kill whom?"

"Sebastian Melstane!"

"I kill Sebastian Melstane?" she cried, rising quickly, and drawing herself up to her full height. "Who dares to accuse me of such a thing?"

"Judas!"

"That wretch?"

"Yes; but you are innocent; I know you are innocent."

"Why?"

"Because I love you!"

Judith looked down at the man kneeling at her feet with a look of infinite gratitude in her eyes, and passed her hand caressingly over his dishevelled hair.

"Poor boy, how true you are! You are willing to believe in my innocence without my denial."

"I am!"

She sat down, again, caught his head between her two hands and kissed him softly on the forehead. As she did so, he felt a hot tear fall on his cheek, and when he looked at her she was crying.

"Judith!" he cried, with sudden terror, "you are weeping."

"Yes. May God always send mankind such true hearts as yours!"

"I would be unworthy of your love if I did not believe you before all the lying scoundrels in the world."

"Alas, Don Quixote!"

"But you can explain everything, Judith. I feel certain you can."

"I can explain when I hear your story. At present I know nothing beyond the fact that Monsieur Guinaud has accused me of a vile crime. What does he say?"

Roger, still kneeling by her side, told the story as related to him by Fanks, and at the conclusion eagerly waited for her denial.

She said nothing, but sat in sombre silence, with her eyes fixed beyond his head in a vague, unseeing manner.

"Judith!" he cried, desperately, "do you not hear what I say? This scoundrel says that you visited Melstane at night and

216

put those two pills into the box with the intention of poisoning him."

Still she said nothing, and Roger felt a feeling of horror arise in his breast as he watched her face, so cold, so frozen, so impassive in its fixed calm.

"He has your handkerchief to prove that you were there. Judith, speak!"

All at once the still figure became endowed with life, and with a choking cry she tore herself from his encircling arms, and sprang across the room.

"Judith!"

In a frenzy of dread he leaped up from his kneeling position, and went rapidly towards her with outstretched hands.

"Stop!" she cried, wildly, shrinking against the wall, "stop!"

"Speak, speak! You must speak and deny this story."

"I cannot."

"Judith."

"I cannot!"

"My God!" he said, in a hoarse whisper, "is it true?"

"I cannot answer you."

Roger felt the room spin round him, and, reeling back, caught at a chair for support, while he gazed with horror-filled eyes at the woman he loved, standing there so rigid and speechless.

"Judith, you do not mean what you say," he cried

217

entreatingly, "you cannot understand. Judas says you murdered Melstane. He can prove it, he says, by the handkerchief. He has told Fanks, who is a detective. You are in danger. I cannot save you. Great Heaven! if you have any pity for me—if you have any pity for yourself, speak and give the lie to this foul accusation."

"I cannot, I tell you, Roger, I cannot!"

"You are innocent!"

"I cannot say."

"Are you guilty?"

"I cannot say."

Axton passed his hand over his brow in a bewildered fashion, hardly knowing if he were asleep or awake, then, with a sudden resolution of despair, flung himself on his knees at her feet.

"Judith! Judith! you must speak, you must. See me kneeling at your feet. I love you, I love you! I do not believe this vile story. In my eyes you are innocent. But the world—think of the world. It will deem you guilty if you cannot defend yourself. Judas has you in his power. He is a merciless wretch. He hates you. He will drag you down to infamy and disgrace, unless you can clear yourself of this crime. Speak for your own sake—for mine. Do not let this devil triumph over you, for Heaven's sake. Deny his foul lies, and let him be punished as he deserves. Speak, for the love of God, speak!"

Judith said nothing, but the quick panting of her breath, the nervous tremor agitating her frame, and the rapid opening and shutting of her hands showed how she was moved.

"She says nothing," said Axton to himself, as he arose slowly to his feet, "she is silent. What does it mean?"

He made one last effort to induce her to deny the accusation of Judas.

"You will not speak!" he said, in tones of acute anguish. "I have knelt, I have prayed; you are silent. I can do nothing. You are innocent, I'll swear; but I cannot prove it. No one can prove it but yourself, and you say nothing. Judith, listen! You are in deadly peril. Fanks is coming up to-night with Judas, and they will accuse you of this crime!"

"To-night?"

"Yes; they have written to Mr. Marson. They will produce the handkerchief. They will tell the story. You refuse to answer me; you must answer them. Fanks told me of this to-day, and I came up at once to warn you."

"It is useless! I can say nothing."

"You must say something. It is a question of life and death. The affair is in the hands of the law. Nothing can save you but your own denial. You must prove the falseness of this horrible story. It means disgrace. It means prison! It means death!"

She looked up suddenly as he spoke those last words, and crossing over to him, laid her hand on his shoulder, speaking wildly, and with uncontrollable agitation.

"I know what it means. You need not tell me that. I know it means the smirching of my fair fame as a woman, I know that it condemns me to an ignominious death; but I can say nothing. Roger, on my soul, I can say nothing. I cannot say I am innocent; I dare not say I am guilty. I must be silent. I must be dumb. Let them say what they like; let them do what they like; my honour and my life rest in the hands of God, and He alone can save me."

"But you are innocent!"

She burst into tears.

"Oh, why do you torture me like this? I tell you I can say nothing; not even to you. My lips are sealed. Let them come up to-night; let them accuse me; let them drag me to prison. I can say nothing. For days, for nights I have dreaded this, now it has come at last. You believe me innocent, my true-hearted lover, but the world will believe me guilty. Let them do so. God knows my sufferings. God knows my anguish, and in His hands I leave myself for good or ill."

He heard her with bowed head, and at the end of her speech he felt a soft kiss on his hair. When he looked up the room was empty.

"Judith!"

There was no reply, and the only sound he heard was the distant slamming of a door that seemed to his agonised imagination to separate him from the woman he loved—for ever.

Chapter 17

220

Francis Marson was considerably perplexed at receiving a note from Fanks, asking for an interview. He guessed at once that Judas had broken faith and unbosomed himself to the detective, but what puzzled him was the reason the Frenchman had for such betrayal. In order to secure the success of his schemes, it was necessary that he should keep silent, yet he had evidently voluntarily revealed his secret knowledge, and thus rendered it useless to himself and his designs. The only way in which Marson could account for the detective's request was that he must have learned the secret of Judas, otherwise there would be no reason why he should seek an interview.

Filled with this idea, Marson summoned up all his courage, and prepared to meet the coming storm with as brave a front as possible. He wrote to Fanks, and told him he would be prepared to see him at eight o'clock that night; then he shut himself up in his study for the rest of the day. Plunged in gloomy reflections, he saw no one, not even Judith; but as the hour approached when he expected his visitor to arrive he was unable to bear his trial in solitude any longer, so, sending for Judith, he told her about the interview. To his surprise, she received the communication with great equanimity, and being in ignorance of her forewarning by Roger, he could not but admire the undaunted spirit with which she was prepared to face the terrible trouble coming to them both.

On her side, Judith saw plainly that Marson was almost distracted by nervous terror and dread of the impending evil, so she did not think it wise to reveal to him the dangerous position in which she was placed. He would

221

learn it in due time; but, meanwhile, she preserved a gloomy silence, and told her adopted father that she would be by his side during the ordeal, in order to support him to the best of her ability. Poor soul, she knew how futile that support would be, but with stern self-repression kept her forebodings locked in her own heart, and Francis Marson felt to a great extent comforted in knowing that he had at least one friend to stand by him in the hour of peril.

It was nearly eight o'clock when Judith entered the study, and found Marson seated at his writing-table, with his gray head buried in his arms. A spasm of agony distorted the calm of her face as she saw the abject terror of the old man; however, repressing all signs of emotion, she moved slowly across the room, and touched him tenderly on the shoulder. He looked up with a startled cry, but was somewhat reassured by the peacefulness of her expression. No marble statue in its eternal calm looked so void of passion and human fear as this tall, pale woman who masked the anguish of her aching heart under an impassive demeanour. Every emotion, every pang, every terror was expressed on the withered countenance of the old man; but she was cold, expressionless, still, as if all human feeling had been frozen in her soul.

Their eyes met for a moment, and from the dim eyes of the man, from the splendid eyes of the woman, there leapt forth a sudden look of mutual dread, of mutual anguish, and horrible suspense. That look spoke all, and they had no need of words to explain their feelings, so Judith sat down near the fire, and Marson resumed his chair at the desk in ominous silence.

At last Marson spoke, low and timidly, as if he feared his words would be trumpeted forth to the four quarters of the world.

"Is Florry better?"

"No, I think she is worse to-night. Very excitable and restless."

"Oh, Judith! Was it wise of you to leave her?"

"She is in good hands. Dr. Japix is with her."

"Japix!" repeated the old man, starting. "I'm sorry about that. On this night of all nights I wish no one in the house!"

"It doesn't matter," replied Judith, feigning an indifference she was far from feeling; "what we know to-night all the world will know to-morrow."

"Good heavens, I hope not!"

"We can expect nothing else from such a man as Judas."

"You mean Guinaud."

"I mean Judas! The name suits such a traitor."

"But why should he act as he is doing?"

"I don't know."

"It is against his own interests."

"Heaven only knows what he considers to be his interests," said Judith, bitterly, "but anything is better than that he should marry Florry!"

"Do you think he would consent to take money instead?"

"I think it's too late to offer any terms. Remember, to-night we deal with the law."

"But Fanks is a friend of Roger Axton."

Judith shuddered, and covered her face with her hands.

"Yes, I know he is," she said, in a low voice; "but Roger can do nothing to help us."

"Are you sure?"

"Quite sure. He told me so this afternoon."

"You saw him?"

"I did!"

Marson was about to speak, but the sombre expression of her face forbade him to ask further questions, and he remained silent.

The minutes seemed to fly by on wings of lightning to this unhappy man and woman, who waited with shuddering dread for the approach of that horror from which they could not escape.

A knock at the door, and then Marks flung it wide open, announcing three visitors.

"Mr. Fanks, Mr. Axton, Monsieur Guinaud."

"Roger," said Judith to herself, with a sudden pang at her heart, as the servant retired. "Oh, the humiliation!"

Marson greeted his three visitors with a grave bow, and they all sat down in silence. There was a sullen look on the face of Judas, for he felt that he had been undiplomatic in his dealings with the detective, and that all his well-laid schemes would come to naught now that his secret was made known.

On the other hand, Fanks appeared serenely confident that things were going as he wished them, but an uneasy expression on his face as he glanced furtively at Judith, showed that he was by no means pleased with the unexpected discovery he had made. Roger said nothing, but sat looking at the carpet with downcast eyes, the very picture of misery and despair.

"You wish to see me, I understand from your letter, sir," said Marson to the detective, in a dull, hopeless voice.

"Yes; with regard to the death of Sebastian Melstane."

"I know nothing about his death."

"Nothing?" repeated Fanks, with great emphasis.

Mr. Marson flushed all over his worn face, and he glanced rapidly at Judith, then repeated his former denial with great deliberation.

"I know nothing about his death."

"Do you know anything, Miss Varlins?"

"I? how should I know?"

"I'm sorry to speak rudely to a lady," said Fanks, suavely, "but this is equivocation."

She looked despairingly at him with the expression of a trapped animal in her eyes, a mute appeal for mercy, but the detective steeled his heart against her, and spoke plainly:

"Do you remember a visit you paid the late Mr. Melstane at Binter's boarding-house during the early part of the month of November?"

"No, I do not."

"Do you recognise this handkerchief?" said Octavius, holding it out to her.

"No. It is a lady's white handkerchief. How should I recognise it?"

"By the name in the corner."

She glanced rapidly at the embroidery, and seeing the fatal name "Judith," let her head fall on her breast with a gesture of despair.

"Do you recognise the handkerchief now?" asked Fanks, with merciless deliberation.

"Yes! It is mine!"

"Do you know where it was found?"

"No!"

"It was found in the sitting-room of Mr. Melstane by this gentleman," said Octavius, pointing to Judas.

She raised her eyes, and her glance followed the direction of his outstretched finger. Hate, contempt, dread, and defiance were all expressed in that rapid look, and Judas shrank back with a feeble smile from the scathing scorn in her eyes.

"This being the case, Miss Varlins," resumed Fanks, coolly, "it is useless for you to deny that you were at Binter's boarding-house on the night in question."

"I do deny it!" she said, resolutely. "I was not at Binter's any night during November; I never saw Mr. Melstane during November. I know nothing about his death!"

Octavius laid the handkerchief on the table with a resolute expression.

"I see I must refresh your memory, Miss Varlins," he said, coolly. "Sebastian Melstane died at Jarlchester on the 13th of November by taking, in all innocence, a morphia pill, which was placed among certain tonic pills he was in the habit of taking. When I find the person who placed the two morphia pills in the box I find the murderer of Sebastian Melstane. Monsieur Guinaud will now resume the story."

Monsieur Judas bowed his head gracefully, and spoke slowly in his vile English.

"At the nights before my frien' Melstane go to Jarlcesterre une dame find him chez lui. I at de vinda stay and overt mes yeux. Mon ami, ce cher Sebastian does go from ze appartement an' zen behold moi ze dame plaze dans un boite à pilules quelque chose, je ne sais quoi."

"Speak English, if you please," said Fanks, sharply.

"Eh, c'est difficile, mais oui. She puts in ze boxes somezing, I knows no wat; zen mon cher ami come again an' ze leave par la fenêtre. I do look after zem, an' see ze mouchoir now wis Monsieur Fanks. Dat is all I speak. La voila."

Roger, who had hitherto kept silent during the whole of this scene, so terrible in its intensity, now sprang to his feet with a cry of rage.

"It's a lie—a lie!" he said, savagely. "Fanks! Marson! you surely don't believe this man—this vile wretch who would sell his soul for money? He killed Melstane himself—I am sure of it!—and tells this lie to ruin an innocent woman and to save his own worthless life. Look at him, all of you? The spy—the traitor—the defamer—the poisoner."

Judas was standing by his chair, breathing heavily, with his face a ghastly white, and his eyes narrowed to their most dangerous expression. So vile, so craven, so treacherous he looked, that all present involuntarily shrank from him with loathing.

"Monsieur!" he said, in his sibilant voice, speaking rapidly in his own tongue, to which he always reverted when excited, "you are a liar and a fool! I did not kill my friend. Bah! I mock myself of that accusation. Think you that I would be here, if I was what you say? What I speak is the truth of the great God! What I declare, I saw! My friend died by the devil-thought of a woman. And that woman is there!"

He pointed straight at Judith, with a long, lean, cruel hand, and the eyes of all, leaving his tall, slim figure, rested on Judith Varlins. She stood still and mute as if she were turned to a statue of stone, and for the space of a minute not a movement was made by any of the actors in this strange drama.

"What do you say to this accusation, Miss Varlins?" asked Fanks, in a tone of deep pity.

"I say nothing."

The words dropped slowly from her white lips, and then the overstrained nerves of the woman gave way, and with a low moan of acute anguish, she sank down in a faint on the floor. Roger sprang forward and raised her in his arms, but Judas, with a mocking, sardonic laugh, tossed his long arms in the air, and burst out into a jeering speech.

"Yes, yes! Take her in your arms! Lift her from the ground, but you cannot lift her again to her purity of a woman. She is lost, the woman you loved. In her place you find the murderess. Ah! it is a good play!"

This cowardly triumphing was too much even for the phlegmatic Fanks, and with a suppressed oath he strode up to the gibing villain.

"If you say another word, you despicable blackguard, I will kill you!"

The Frenchman turned on him with the snarling ferocity of a tiger.

"Eh, you will kill me, my brave! Is it that I am a child you can rage at with your big words? Miserable English that you are, I spit upon you! I, Jules Guinaud, laugh at your largeness. Eh! I believe well. You are afraid of what I say; but I keep not the silence, holy blue! Bah! your sweet English lady, she is a criminal!"

"You lie!" shouted Roger, madly, starting to his feet. "You lie, you wretch! Marson! Fanks! Get me some water! She has fainted. And as for you, scoundrel—"

He advanced towards Judas with clenched fists, whereupon the Frenchman, with a look of fear on his gray face, recoiled against the wall. But not even the threatening attitude of the young man could restrain the gibing devil that possessed this villain, and with a shrill scream of laughter he went on with his insults.

"For me the box, monsieur. But certainly, you are wise—you are very wise. Come, now, if you are bold—I hide not the truth, I declare—if your angel is not the one who killed the dear Melstane, say, who is it? Declare the name."

Roger, with glittering eyes, and a fierce look on his face, would have sprung on Judas and caught him by the throat, when the answer to the question came from a most unexpected quarter.

Outside the room there was a shrill scream, the heavy tramping of feet, and a woman in her nightgown dashed madly into their midst.

It was Florry Marson!

In her eyes shone the fever of insanity, on her dry lips a fearful laugh of horrible laughter, and she whirled round and round in the middle of the room like a Maenad, while Japix, who had followed her, tried vainly to approach.

"God! How like her mother!"

The cry of horror came from the lips of Marson, who was holding a glass of water to the lips of Judith; but his daughter did not hear him. With a shriek she stopped her insensate whirling, and dashed forward with distorted features to Monsieur Judas.

"Hold her! hold her!" cried Japix, "she is mad—raving."

Judas was too terrified to do anything, and stood nerveless and paralysed, facing this ghastly spectre with the loose hair, the frantic gestures, and blazing eyes.

"What have you done with him?" shrieked Florry, making futile clutches at Judas, "you fiend! you reptile! Why did I not kill you instead of Sebastian?"

A cry of horror burst from the lips of the listeners.

"Give him to me! give him to me!" howled the mad woman, "you know I killed him! I did not mean it! I did not mean it! The devil told me about the morphia. Hist! I will tell you! His name is Spolger. He lives in the big house on the hill. He has poison. Oh, yes, yes! I know. I stole it to give Sebastian—poor Sebastian."

"Gentlemen," cried Marson, piteously, "do not believe her. This is raving."

"I believe it's the truth," said Fanks, solemnly.

Japix advanced towards Florry, but she saw him coming, and with a shriek of anger, darted towards the study table, upon which she sprang with the activity of an antelope. Her foot touched the lamp, it fell over, and in a moment the fierce flame had caught her light draperies, and she stood before the horrified spectators a pillar of flame.

"I burn! I burn!" she screamed. "Sebastian, help! help! it is my punishment! It is—God! God! save me—save me."

Roger tore down one of the curtains and ran to her

assistance, but she bounded off the table, and running to Judas flung her arms round his neck. With a yell of terror he tried to fling her off, but she only clung the closer, and the flames caught his clothes.

"Save me, Sebastian, I did not mean to kill you. Ah, ah!"

"Mon Dieu, help me!"

Both Fanks and Roger flung themselves on the writhing pair, who were now rolling on the floor, and they managed to extinguish the flames. Florry was terribly burnt, and the Frenchman had fainted. Old Marson on his knees was praying feebly, and Judith, recovering from her stupor, rose slowly up.

"What is the matter?"

The answer came in a wailing voice from the brokenhearted father:

"The judgment of God! The judgment of God!"

Extracts From a Detective's Note-Book

"I am utterly dumbfounded . . . Judith is innocent . . . She is a noble woman, and Florry, the martyr, who loved Melstane so, is his murderess . . . The little serpent . . . But let me speak as kindly of her as I can . . . She is dead . . . A terrible death . . . Well might her old father say it was the judgment of God . . . The sight was terrible . . . I shall never be able to get it out of my thoughts . . . Strange how the discovery was made . . . And that noble Judith Varlins was going to bear the burden of her adopted sister's sin . . . What a woman . . . If I envy Roger anything I envy him the splendid heroine he is going to make his wife . . . I take back with shame and regret all that I have said against her in this book . . . She is a noble woman, and Florry—well, she is dead, so I will say nothing! 'De mortuis,' etc.

"*Mem.*—To ask Japix, Roger, Spolger, and Judas to meet me at some place in order to learn precisely how the crime was committed . . . I should have been spared all this wrongful suspicion of innocent people if Judas had told me the truth . . . He knew all along who committed the crime, and was trading on the knowledge for his own ends . . . I should have thought that even he would have hesitated before marrying a murderess . . . but it was her money he wanted . . . No doubt he laughs at the way I have blundered—well, I deserve it . . . I have acted very wrongly in a great number of ways; but I would defy any one but a detective in a 'novel' to have unravelled this strange case . . . The mystery was revealed by no mortal, but by God. . .

"Under these circumstances I can afford to bear the gibes of Monsieur Judas in silence. . ."

Chapter 18

How It Was Done

Three days after that terrible night, five men were seated in the study of Dr. Japix talking over the series of strange events which began with the death of Sebastian Melstane by poison, and ended with the death of Florry Marson by fire. These five men were:

Dr. Jacob Japix, M.D.; Mr. Octavius Fanks, detective; Roger Axton, Esq., gentleman; Jackson Spolger, Esq., manufacturer; Monsieur Jules Guinaud, chemist's assistant.

It was about midday; the world outside was white with snow, the sky was heavy with sombre clouds, and these five men, actors in the drama known as the Jarlchester Mystery, had met together in order to explain their several shares in the same.

Octavius Fanks had described the manner in which he had first become involved in the affair, the methods by which he had traced the crime, and the reasons he had had for his several suspicions.

At the conclusion of the detective's speech Roger Axton took up the thread of the story, supplying by oral testimony all the points of which Fanks was ignorant. Having finished his story, Monsieur Judas arose to his feet and revealed all he knew about the case.

"But first, my friends," he said, with venomous malignity, "I give to Monsieur Fanks the congratulations on his talent for foolish fancies. Eh! yes, he is a grand detective, this young man, who thinks all have committed the murder but the real one. Conceive to yourselves, messieurs, the blindness of this monsieur—"

"I admit all your abuse," interrupted Fanks, curtly; "go on with what you have to tell."

"Eh! I enrage this monsieur, me," said Judas, with an

insolent laugh. "Bah! I mock myself of his anger. Behold, messieurs, I tell you the little tale of all things. Me, I loved this angel that now is dead; but she her heart gave to the dear Melstane. She returned from the Île de Vight and tells Melstane that her father is poor, and she is to marry this amiable Spolgers. My friend Melstane is enraged, and says: 'I go to your father to tell him I wish you for mine.' But the dear angel is afraid of the hard poverty. She weeps, she entreats, she implores the cruel Melstane to release her, but he refuses with scorn. Myself I heard it all. She speaks to me as her friend. I paint her the pictures of starving, I make her to shrink with fear. Conceive, I implore you, messieurs, how this beautiful one, reared in money, dreads the coldness of the poor. She says: 'He must not drag me to poorness! I am afraid of myself if he does. I am like my mother.' Then, messieurs, I hear from her sweet lips that madame, her dead mother, was mad. The poor angel is afraid she will be mad some day also. Nevertheless, I love her, I wish her for mine. I am the friend of Melstane; but him I love not, because of this dear one. I say: 'My friend Melstane will pull you to the cold, to the street, to the want of bread. Defend yourself, my beautiful. Kill him!'"

"Oh!" cried Roger, in a tone of horror, "you put the idea into her head?"

"Eh! I say she was mad like madame, her mother. I told her of the starvation; oh, but yes, certainly, I did say to her: 'Mademoiselle, if he lives, you will be taken to poorness. Kill him!' What would you, messieurs? I but say to her what myself I would do if in the same way. My suggestion with fear she received, and went weeping away. But again she sees the dear Melstane, and he tells her he will speak to her father. She implores, she kneels, but he is hard stone. I wish to have all the place to myself, so as to love this angel, and to Melstane I say: 'Go thou, my friend, to some town and tell the angel to follow thee. Then you can demand of monsieur the father what you will. He is enchanted, this dear Melstane, and to me speaks with pleasure: 'Eh, but the idea is too beautiful! This I will do, and if the father has any of the money, thou, my friend, will be to me as a brother.' When next he meets the dear child, he tells her of the plan. It is that he is to depart to Jarlcesterre, and there when writes he, she is to come. She says this she will do, but I, messieurs, eh! I smile to myself. In her heart she hates where once she loved. She has fear of the poorness. She says: 'I will myself kill this cruel one, and no one will know of him dying.' Behold, then, on the night before goes the dear Melstane, she comes to the pension. Myself I see her; I wait at the window and behold. She demands from my Sebastian what he has not, and to obtain it he goes from the apartment. Then in the box of pills on the table she places something. What I know not then, but now I am aware, it is the pills of morphia!"

"Which you gave her, I suppose?" said Fanks, disgusted with the callous manner in which the scoundrel spoke.

"Monsieur is wrong. The truth of the great God I now tell, and I know not where she obtained the death-pills."

"I can explain that," interrupted Spolger, quickly.

"Eh, truly, you were then more of the evil to the dear angel than myself. Well, messieurs, I repeat my story. The dear Melstane departs for Jarlcesterre, and I am free to love the angel; but I speak to her not. I see her not, I wait for the time to speak. One says she is to be the bride of the rich Spolgers. Eh, I laugh, but nothing I say to any one. Then by the mistake of the office of post I do receive the letters sent by this Monsieur Axton to Mees Varlins. I at first refuse, but when I behold I see the mark of Jarlcesterre and open the letters. In them this I discover."

He threw a folded paper which he was holding in his hand on the table, and Fanks, opening it quickly, gave a cry of surprise.

"A marriage certificate!"

It certainly was, stating that a marriage had taken place in October between Sebastian Melstane, bachelor, and Florence Marson, spinster, at a registry office in London.

"Yes!" said Judas, complacently, "it is that the dear angel was married to my friend Melstane. Conceive then, messieurs, why she killed him with the poison. He had the right to take her to the poorness. She was afraid because of my speech, and as no hope of help beheld she, this foolish one goes to the extremes and kills the man who holds her. Eh, messieurs, when this I see, I know I do hold the angel in my power. Then clever Monsieur Fanks arrives and tells me of the death. He speaks of the pills, and as in a moment behold I that Mees Mar-rson has poisoned the husband she feared. I admire; eh, truly, it was a great thing for a woman thus to behave. Then to myself I spoke. 'Jules Guinaud, with this you hold, it is for you to be the husband of the widow Melstane.'"

"For Heaven's sake don't call her that name," said Roger, with a shudder.

"Wherefore not, monsieur? She was of a certainty the widow Melstane, and her husband she killed. I go then to Monsieur Mar-rson; I show the certificate of marriage; I tell of the death. To him I speak: 'If I marry not your daughter I betray all to the law.' He shudders with the fear and says: 'You will be my son-in-law.' Then comes Mees Judith, who knows of my love; but her I quickly crush. Eh, it was very well; but she played the traitor to me, so to her I also was cruel. I tell this dear Monsieur Fanks that she is the criminal, and show him the handkerchief of her which was let to fall by the dear angel. We go to the house of Monsieur Mar-rson, and then the angel is distraught; she is mad and tells all. Behold, messieurs, my story is at an end, and nothing can I say more. I played for a large thing. I have lost. It is cruel, but who can fight the angry gods? Everything I have failed in. All are innocent but the angel, and she is dead. But I have held her in my arms. Yes, though the flames did burn, she was to me for a moment, so I am satisfied. Behold, then, all is at an end, and Jules Guinaud to you, messieurs, says 'Adieu.'"

Monsieur Judas resumed his seat in a conscious manner, as if he expected a round of applause for his very dramatic delivery of his villainous narrative. If he did expect praise he was disappointed, for a chorus of execration burst from the four men who had listened so patiently to this infamous history.

"You scoundrel!"

"Fiend!"

"Wretch!"

"Blackguard!"

Judas was not at all dismayed, but shrugged his shoulders and smiled.

"Eh, messieurs les Tartuffes, I make you the compliments. If you had been as me, acted the same you would have, I think. But all I have told, and now will the dear Spolger tell us of the pills which he gave to the angel?"

"I did not give her pills, you wicked wretch," said Spolger, vehemently. "I was as much in the dark as you about the cause of Melstane's death. The whole affair has been a great blow to me. I do not know when my nerves will recover."

"Will you tell us your story, Mr. Spolger?" said Fanks, politely.

"Certainly; if only to disabuse your mind of the suspicions put into it by that infernal scoundrel there."

The Frenchman, at whom this compliment was pointed, threw an ugly look at the millionaire which foreboded anything but good to that gentleman's well-being, but with his accustomed presence of mind soon recovered himself with an enigmatic smile.

"My faith, this 'dear Spolgers' is a tragedy of one act. Is it not so?"

"No, it isn't," retorted Mr. Spolger, tartly; "and now, as you've given your version of the story, perhaps you'll permit me to tell mine to these gentlemen, and clear myself from your vile insinuations."

Judas nodded his red head with a mocking smile, and Mr. Spolger, after glancing at him viciously, immediately explained himself.

"The whole affair is this," he said, in his peevish voice. "Miss Marson was up at my house before Melstane went to Jarlchester, and displayed considerable curiosity about the manufacture of the 'Spolger Soother,' which you no doubt know is a pill meant to soothe the nerves and give a good night's rest. I was willing to show Miss Varlins all the attention possible, and therefore made up some pills for her with my own hands, to show her how it was done. As there is morphia in the pills, I weighed out the requisite quantity with great care, upon which she asked me if I made a mistake and put in too much, what would be the result. I told her that in such a case the person would probably die. Upon which she made a remark which struck me as curious then, but which does not strike me as curious now. She said: 'If, then, you made one pill with too much morphia in it, the person taking it would die, and even if the rest of the pills were examined, no reason could be given for his death.' I assured her that this would probably be the case, but said that all our 'Soothers' were manufactured in a most careful manner. After this she manifested no further interest in the pills being made, so I sealed up the jar of morphia and placed it on the shelf. Shortly afterwards, I was called out of the room, and was absent for about a quarter of an hour; so I've no doubt that in my absence the unhappy girl took some morphia out of the bottle—if you remember, Mr. Fanks, the seal was broken—and carrying it home with her, made the two fatal pills according to the method I had shown her. These pills she afterwards—according to the story of Monsieur Judas—placed in the box of tonic pills left by Melstane on the table. Down at Jarlchester he took one and died; the other, I understand from Mr. Fanks, was analysed by Dr. Japix, and found to contain a great deal of morphia. I am afraid, therefore, that in all innocence I contributed to the catastrophe of Melstane's death. I beg to state, however, that there is this difference between myself and Monsieur Guinaud. He put the idea willingly into her head to kill Melstane. I showed her how, but inadvertently; so I am confident, gentlemen, that you will admit that no blame attaches to me in the affair."

"Of course not," said Japix, emphatically, when Spolger had

finished; "what you did, you did in all innocence. For my part, I look upon Monsieur Judas as culpable."

"Eh, truly," said Judas, with a sneer, "and for why, monsieur? I did not kill the dear Melstane."

"No; but you put the idea of killing him into Miss Marson's head!"

"That is not guilt, monsieur."

"Not legally, certainly, but morally!"

"Name of names! I care not for your morals, me. The law cannot touch me, so I laugh at your reproach."

"Nevertheless, Monsieur Judas," said Fanks, meaningly, "I would recommend you to leave Ironfields as soon as possible!"

"And for why? No one knows of this affair. Is it not so?"

"Of course! But though your character is not known to the world, it is to me. I am the law, and the law shall force you to leave this place. A man like you is dangerous, so you had better go back to your Paris, where you will find a few congenial scoundrels like yourself!"

"Eh, monsieur! I have no wish to stay in this rain climate," said Judas, scoffingly; "but if I chose to stay I would, certainly!"

"Try," said Fanks, significantly,

But Monsieur Judas had no wish to try. He simply shrugged his shoulders, and intimated that if they had learned all they desired from him, he was anxious to depart. Roger, however, asked him to resume his seat.

241

"I think it is only just to state the part taken by Miss Varlins in this lamentable affair," he said, quietly. "She had no idea that Miss Marson had anything to do with the death of Melstane for a long time. She asked me to obtain the letters from Melstane, thinking that he might use them to create a scandal, but she did not know that the certificate of marriage was among them. When, however, Miss Marson was ill, she betrayed the fact of the marriage and the existence of a certificate in her delirium. Miss Varlins was anxious to keep the fact of the marriage quiet, as, seeing Melstane was now dead, the whole affair might blow over. This was the reason she refused to let Mr. Fanks see the letters without her first looking through them, as she thought he might discover the marriage certificate and connect Miss Marson indirectly with the death of her miserable husband. Of the horrible truth, however, she had no idea till later on, when Miss Marson, in her sick-bed ravings, betrayed the whole affair. She then acted in a manner befitting her noble nature. The dead girl, gentlemen, was left to Miss Varlins as a sacred charge by the late Mrs. Marson, and Miss Varlins proved herself worthy of the trust. She resolved to stand between the guilty woman and the law, even at the cost of ignominy and disgrace to herself. I implored her to tell me the truth, never for a moment deeming her guilty. She refused to answer my questions, she refused to either deny or affirm the accusation, and it was then I guessed she was shielding some one; but I never thought it was Florry Marson; I thought it was her father. Now, gentlemen, the mystery is cleared up—the riddle is guessed. Florry Marson murdered the unhappy man who died at Jarlchester; but had it not been for the accident of her escaping from her sick-room and revealing her guilt in her delirium, Miss Varlins would have had to bear the stigma of this crime. A noble woman, gentlemen, you must all of you confess."

242

"Noble indeed," assented all present, except Judas, who laughed quietly to himself.

"In a few months," resumed Roger, his voice trembling, "I hope to lead her to the altar as my wife, and I pray to God that the brightness of the future will make amends for the sorrows of the past, and that I may prove worthy of this pearl of womanhood which I hope soon to have in my keeping."

"Amen!" said Japix, in his deep voice. "And now one word more. Florry Marson is dead, so of her let us speak kindly. It is true she killed Melstane; but, gentlemen, she was guiltless of the crime in one sense. Her mother, a shallow, frivolous woman, was insane with a suicidal mania, and several times tried to destroy herself. She died, mad—raving mad, and the insanity in her blood descended to her unhappy daughter. Hence the reason of Miss Varlins' great care and watchfulness. She was aware that the seeds of a homicidal mania were in the blood of the happy, laughing girl, and might develop when least expected. They developed, gentlemen, when she received a shock from the conduct of Melstane. He had thought her rich; then he found she was poor, and instead of making the best of it, as any honourable man would have done, he threatened her until her delicately poised brain went off the balance. Even then, however, she might have been saved from the crime, had she been left alone. But the idea of murder was placed in her mind by the respectable Guinaud, and once there, it soon took shape. With the usual cunning of mad people, she resolved to commit the crime with as little danger to herself as possible. No idea of how to do it, however, occurred to her mind until her unfortunate conversation with Mr. Spolger, in which he showed her the way."

"In all innocence," interrupted Spolger, hastily.

243

"Of course, in all innocence," replied Japix, gravely. "Once having the idea of how to do it in her head, she put it into execution. She made the pills and watched her opportunity to place them in the box unknown to Melstane. How she managed it you know from the story of Monsieur Judas; but I am certain that if Melstane had shown her a little kindness, a little forbearance, she would have relented at the last moment. She was not altogether mad; she hardly knew what she was doing, and it was only when she heard suddenly of Melstane's death that the full enormity of her crime struck her. What was the result, gentlemen? It sent her mad—raving mad. She died, as we know, terribly, but even such a death was a blessing in disguise, for she would never have recovered her reason, and would have died in a madhouse."

Every one present having thus given his evidence, Fanks summarized the whole affair in a few shorthand notes in his secretive little pocket-book.

"When Florry Marson married Sebastian Melstane, she was sane. The seeds of insanity were in her blood, but had not developed.

"Owing to the brutal treatment of her husband and the suggestions of Judas, the hereditary disease became manifested in her in the form of a homicidal mania.

"The conversation with Jackson Spolger showed her a method by which she could kill her now hated husband at small risk to herself.

"She took advantage of it, made the pills with morphia stolen from Spolger's bottle, and placed the pills in the box during a visit to Binter's boarding-house.

244

"Melstane went down to Jarlchester to await her arrival, and took the pill in all innocence. The sudden news of his death upset the balance of her brain and sent her mad.

"From such madness she could never have recovered, so it was most merciful that she died."

The Jarlchester Mystery thus having been solved, Fanks replaced his note-book in his pocket, and the company prepared to break up. The first to go was Monsieur Judas, who stood at the door, hat in hand, smiling blandly on the four Englishmen.

"Messieurs," said Judas, in his most suave voice, "I make you my best compliments on your brains. You have been all in the dark. I, Jules Guinaud, showed you the light, and with brutal behaviour you have spoken to me. The dear angel is dead, my friend Melstane is dead, so now I leave this foggy climate of yours for my dear France. You have not the politeness, you English! You are all coarse of the style of your bifsteak. Bah! I mock myself of you! But I say no more. Adieu, messieurs, adieu! The politeness of the accomplished French survives the brutality of the bulldog English! Adieu! and for a good-bye English: Damn you all, messieurs!"

And the accomplished Judas, beaten on every point, but polite to the end, vanished from the room, and later on from Ironfields itself.

Chapter 19

. . . I had quite intended to duly label this note-book, and put it away among my papers, but somehow I forgot to do so, and only came across it the other day by accident. I have been reading the Jarlchester Mystery over again, and it struck me as one of the most extraordinary cases I have ever had the pleasure of investigating. It is now about a year ago since I left Ironfields after having brought Judas to book, and I am rather pleased at discovering this pocket-book now, as it gives me an opportunity of completing the case by telling his fate . . .

". . . In the *Figaro* of last Monday I read an account of a certain Jules Guinaud, who is none other than my old friend, Monsieur Judas. It appears that after having left Ironfields, the accomplished Judas returned to Paris as offering a wider field for his peculiar talents, and there he married a very wealthy young lady. After the marriage, however, Monsieur Judas found out that his mother-in-law had the money, and it would not descend to the daughter until her death. On discovering this disagreeable state of things, Monsieur Judas proceeded to put his mother-in-law out of the way, and managed to do so by means of his old poison, morphia. Madame Judas inherited the money, monsieur had the handling of it, and all was going well, only monsieur found madame flirting with a good-looking cousin. Filled with virtuous indignation at the violation of the domestic hearth, Monsieur Judas proceeded to poison the cousin, but before he could manage it, madame, remembering the suspicious death of her mother, interfered, and the end of the affair was the recovery of the cousin, the exhumation of the mother-in-law's body, and the arrest of Monsieur Judas . . .

". . . He made a very ingenious defence, but the case was clearly proved against him, and he was sentenced to the guillotine. Monsieur Judas, however, it appears, had some influence in an underhand way, and got his sentence commuted to penal servitude; so now he is on his way to New Caledonia, where he will stay for the rest of his life in congenial company. It is reported that Madame Judas intends to get a divorce, in which case I presume she will marry the good-looking cousin. . . .

". . . Monsieur Judas thus being disposed of, I had better make a note of the present condition of the other actors in the mystery. . . .

". . . After Florry Marson's death her father fell into his dotage. Shortly afterwards his firm became bankrupt; the second blow was too much for him, and he died six months ago. . . .

". . . Roger Axton is married to Judith Varlins, and I envy him his noble wife. They have not much money, but still manage to live moderately well on Roger's income, in a pretty cottage at Hampstead. I dined there last Sunday, and Roger showed me the MS. of his new novel, which is so good that I predict a success. But who can tell if it will be a success? The public? No. The publishers? No. Not even the critics. At all events, Roger and his dear wife are very happy —so happy, indeed, that I think I must follow their example. But where will I find a wife like Judith? . . .

". . . The last I heard of Mr. Spolger was that he had taken up his abode at Malvern to drink the waters. He is still ill, and still trying new medicines. The Soother is selling very largely, and every one takes it—except the proprietor. . . .

". . . As to Japix, well, I saw him two weeks ago, and we had a little conversation over the Jarlchester affair. It arose out of a simple remark of mine. . . .

"'One thing puzzles me,' I said, 'in reference to the Jarlchester case, how such a shallow little piece of frivolity as Florry Marson could carry out her plans so cleverly.'

"'The cunning of madness,' replied Japix, after a pause. 'I told you her mother was mad, and of course it broke out in her. Clever? I should think she was. Do you remember how cleverly she acted about Melstane, saying that she loved him, and all the rest of it, yet all the time she knew he had death in that pill-box?'

"'If she had been a strong-minded woman —'

"'If she had been, my dear boy, she very likely would not have committed the crime. It is your shallow-brained beings that commit most crimes. The least shock sends their weak heads off the balance, and they don't know what they are doing. In this case, however, as I've told you a dozen times, it was hereditary insanity.'

"'A strange case!'

"'A very strange case, and what a noble woman Mrs. Axton is! By the way, how is Mrs. Axton? I've not been to see them yet.'

"'Mrs. Axton,' I replied, solemnly, 'is quite well, but is expecting an interesting event. They are going to call him Octavius after me.'

"Japix roared like a Bull of Bashan.

"'You seem pretty certain about the sex,' he observed, wiping his eyes; 'but fancy calling the first child Octavius, which means eighth. It's like a riddle.'

"'And why not? The whole marriage arose out of a riddle.'

"'How so?'

"'The Jarlchester Mystery.'

"'Well, you've found out your riddle,' said Japix, coolly; 'but, as you can't guess how such a frivolous girl as Florry could commit such a clever murder, it's a riddle to you still.'

"'It is! Let us put it in the form of an epigram.'

"'Proceed.'

"'This is a riddle! Guess it. 'Tis still a riddle!'

"'Humph! Author?'

"'Myself.'

"'I thought so,' said Japix, rudely, and departed."

THE END

www.ingramcontent.com/pod-product-compliance
Lightning Source LLC
Chambersburg PA
CBHW030812020726
47499CB00006B/1886